Our Phantom Voyage

by Patricia Macko

DORRANCE
PUBLISHING CO
EST. 1920
PITTSBURGH, PENNSYLVANIA 15238

Dorrance Publishing Co
585 Alpha Drive
Pittsburgh, PA 15238
Visit our website at *www.dorrancebookstore.com*

ISBN: 978-1-4809-9519-2
eISBN: 978-1-4809-9591-8

In Loving Memory
of My Mother Coletta Flynn

Dedicated to My Sisters
Kitty Flynn Oravec and Mary Flynn Martin

Introduction

For many years this story has been told at family gatherings. Narrated by my sister, who is the main character of this book, it never fails to cause hysterical laughter by those who are hearing it and imagining how the experiences described must have caused frustration, anger, fear, sorrow and happiness for Maggie and Rose.

Based on a true story, this book is sure to have a universal appeal to readers who enjoy adventure, romance and the age old good vs. evil scenario. You will end up cheering on the antics of Maggie and Rose as they uncover and disrupt a drug running operation of the underworld via a cruise vacation that is anything but the luxury and relaxation they thought they signed up for.

This mix of humor, tragedy, and adventure will take you through a voyage of page turning, non-stop interest that will entertain to the very end.

Our Phantom Voyage is based on a true story that has been embellished beyond reality. The names have been changed to protect the guilty. Enjoy!

Chapter One

I don't much like what I'm looking at in the mirror this morning. Here I am squeezing my big arse into a pair of hideous khaki work pants and matching man's button down shirt. I'm wearing a badge on my humungous chest that defines me as a County Corrections Officer. It's my first day of work at the county jail. What am I doing? How did I get here? Oh yeah, I begged for the job. I saw it as a way out of the chrome plating factory that I was working in. It was such a caustic environment there and I was literally tearing the skin off all my fingers on the job I was assigned. Surely the jail will be an improvement over that place. You see, my new brother-in-law was a Deputy Sheriff for the County and he was well connected with the bigwigs. He'd been working down there for six years and he was well known and liked. We all liked him too. Especially Grannie. She always loved a man in uniform. I guess that's why she married one. Anyway, we got to talking at a family get together and he asked me if I wanted him to inquire about a CO position for me. He felt pretty sure he could make that happen. I remember him saying "make sure you want to do this, because if I ask for you, I'm sure you'll get the job." Well, I didn't take any time to think it through and told him immediately that I was sure I would like to work for the County. My dad always told us, "Try to get a government job. The benefits are great and you will always have job security." Without any college behind me, and no real skills, I saw this as an opportunity for me. Turns out, it was.

So here I stand. Dressed and ready for the big day. I think. Out the door and on my way. All the way downtown my stomach is doing flips. I'm so nervous I'm afraid I'm going to be sick. Please God! Not that! For some reason I started thinking about my Grandfather. Grandpa Green. Long passed, but forever remembered. He served the city as a policeman for 30 years. That was back in the days of Eliot Ness. Back in 1935 the Mayor of Cleveland, Harold Hitz Burton, appointed Eliot Ness, Safety Director. At that time, the city was overcome with crime and corruption and the Mayor felt sure that the officer who brought down Al Capone, could clean up the city of Cleveland. Well, he was right! On his watch, Eliot Ness weeded out 200 crooked police officers and brought fifteen city officers to trial for criminal behavior. Before he was done, Cleveland was named Safest City in the United States by the National Safety Council. At one time in his career, Grandpa Green was assigned to the security detail guarding Eliot Ness while he was in the city interviewing with the Mayor. I remember Grandpa telling the story of how he was standing guard in the hotel hallway where Eliot Ness was staying. His job was to keep everyone off the floor so the Ness party had complete privacy. As Grandpa was dutifully standing watch that night, he got the privilege of seeing none other than Eliot himself. Grandpa recalled the story at most of our family parties. It was one of those that never got old and everyone always wanted to hear it again and again. Grandpa Green was one of a kind. He was totally committed to the rules and procedures of the Department, but he was also smart enough to know when it was necessary to look the other way. That night with Eliot Ness was one of those nights. Grandpa not only looked the other way when he saw something he shouldn't have, he did his best to protect the new Safety Director and all his cronies from any outsiders, and especially the press. Grandpa Green was always someone I looked up to. I felt a special connection to him and I loved him so much. I only wished he was still around so I could talk to him about my new job. But I started praying to Grandpa Green for strength and courage. I prayed that whole way down the Shoreway on the way to the County Jail. The sun was shining through the windshield and I felt a warmth inside that felt a bit comforting. It felt familiar and safe. It felt like a hug. I knew who it was that was riding with me that morning. Please stay with me Grandpa. If you can help me get through this first day then I know I can take it from there.

I show up at roll call and faintly answer "here" when Sarge called out my name. I am literally shaking in my size 12's with absolutely no idea of what I'd be doing for the next eight hours. The county's idea of training was throwing you to the wolves' day one. Learn as you go was their philosophy in those days. Of course they've come a long way since then, but there I was that first day, standing in the middle of a female "pod." A pod. What's a pod? That sounded to me like something to do with insects, or critters of some sort. Anyone who knows Maggie Flannery knows that I want nothing to do with critters. Anything with four legs terrifies me. Ever since I was a little girl I've had a phobia about animals. Any kind of animal. A dog crossing my path can paralyze me. The fear overwhelms me to the point of completely losing muscle function. People just do not understand this. The anxiety I suffer when confronted with any sort of animal causes me to completely lose control. I become immobile, speechless, and debilitated. Luckily I am not expecting to confront any animals today. At least not the four legged kind. It was me and 24 female inmates in that pod. How do you like those odds? My stature worked in my favor. Most of these women were typically five feet five inches or shorter. Up against my six foot frame, there weren't many who were brave enough to challenge me. If they knew how scared I was, they could have walked all over me. Fortunately my continuous silence was mistaken for a mean disposition. I had a natural scowl most of the time, so I was quickly sized up as no one to mess with.

The jail had 10 floors. It housed, on average, 1200 inmates. On any given shift, 80 officers were on duty. The windows were narrow, the idea being that a person could not fit through. They were made of security glass and could not be broken. Added to that, there was an iron bar welded across each window on the outside of the building. The Control Room was strategically located in the middle of the floor. There were two hallways of pods on either side. It reminded me of high school. Especially with those tile floors. An Ectacom system was our way of talking to each other and also talking to the Control Room. It was our life line. All doors had one and I made it my business early on to learn how to use it. That was the start of my career as a County Corrections Officer. For whatever strange reason, I seemed to thrive in that job. Inmates were scared of me, staffers respected me, and I quickly earned a reputation as a straight shooter. "By the book" Maggie Flannery. Don't mess with her. I used my strict Catholic upbringing as a guideline for behavior on the job. Don't lie, cheat, or steal, and respect everyone. They will usually respect you back. That mantra worked well for me. Not all my co-workers abided by the same values, but I quickly sorted out those who I could bond with and made quick friends with Tracey, Joan, and Jill. We had each other's backs and we knew we could count on each other in a tough situation. And believe me, we faced a few of those together.

Chapter Two

We'd been waiting a while for the second car in our group to arrive at Tracey's house. Good thing Tracey gave us her extra key to get in the house because we arrived way before she did. It was an ugly February night. The rain hitting the windows was so violent we were afraid to get close enough to look outside. The crack of light in the black sky, followed by the continuous booming of thunder was enough to frighten all of us to the point of alarm. The wind was whipping the oak tree on the front lawn right against the house. It was so powerful. We were not sure the roof could withstand that kind of beating. Tracey's little kitty was hiding under the couch scared to death. I'm not sure what she's more afraid of, us or the storm. For me, it was the kitty. That four legged creature was hiding under the couch. In my mind she was baring her teeth, waiting to pounce. On me. I can't stand it another minute. The fear I feel inside has me about to go outside and wait in the car. I check my watch. It had been over thirty minutes since we left the Mexican res-

taurant and our worry was starting to turn into panic. Where
are they? What's taking so long for them to get here? Then we
heard the sirens over the pelting rain. Tony decides to go back
out into the storm to see if he can find them. There was no way
we would let him go out there without us. The rain is really
coming down now and is freezing immediately on the street.
We could hear the sirens and we followed the sound to try and
find where they were. My heart sank as I realized the reality of
what was happening. I'm trying to control the car but we are
sliding all over on the black ice. I have to slow down a bit for
our own safety sake. Upon arrival at the scene, our worst fears
are confirmed. Tony sees a car smashed into a huge oak tree.
The car is almost unrecognizable but he knows it's Tracey. It's
literally cut in half with the back half landing very close to the
garage of the house they are in front of. The first responders
are working fiercely to somehow pry the girls out of the wreckage. I immediately start praying. It's an automatic response for
me. My mom instilled that in us at a young age. When you see
someone hurt or in trouble, start praying. Holy Mother of God,
please help us!

Chapter Three

Tracey was driving that night. We all called her Hollywood. At five foot two and 110 pounds, she was the showgirl of the group. With a set of double D's, a 22" waist, and the face of an angel, she had it all. Her ex-husband, Tony, just could not get over her. Even though they'd been divorced for five years now, he never lost hope that somehow, someway, they would get back together. He stayed totally devoted to her and would do anything for her. Her, not so much!

We were all good people. We worked hard, stayed honest. We all really needed some time off to get away from the tension and anxiety of our everyday working lives.

The guilt was beginning to set in. I could not help feeling this was all my fault somehow. The pre-vacation celebration was all for me. It was my birthday and they just could not let it go uncelebrated. We ended up a group of twenty for the birthday dinner. We decided on ChiChi's, one of our favorite Mexican restaurants. The strawberry marguerites were going down smooth and the tortilla chips and salsa just kept on coming. We all had a great dinner and then, of course, I could not escape without the wearing of the huge Mexican sombrero and the gang of waiters leading the group in their version of Happy Birthday. We did have a great time and everyone got the chance to have some fun and blow off a little steam. So I had to be the victim of their sarcasm and humor for the night. I could take it. Hey, why not. We were leaving the next morning for sunny beaches and umbrella drinks. We couldn't wait!

When Tony discovered the accident, there was no stopping him from running up to the wreckage. The police on the scene told him to wait. The EMT's were on their way. Tony wasn't waiting. He nearly fainted when he got there and saw her. Twisted, pinned down, and bleeding profusely. He immediately went into action. He was not a medical professional, but he had enough first aid training to know how to help. He would do anything to save her. Tony was focused on Tracey. So much so, that he barely noticed the passenger.

It was Jill, one of Tracey's best friends and co-workers. Jill was also divorced, but she would not let her ex near her. She was a victim of domestic violence and had a very bitter taste of marriage. The wedded bliss she experienced was more blisters than bliss. She was set free by her divorce and was determined to start living the life she longed for. It was Jill's idea to go on the cruise. She wanted adventure, fun, and new experiences in her life. She was the organizer and coordinator of the trip for us. She had the skill set and good common sense to manage the logistics and details. Jill was outspoken and very opinionated. Not the least bit shy. At the age of 42, she was still very attractive. With reddish-brown hair, she had the bluest eyes you've ever seen. The kind of eyes guys got lost in. She had power over men, and yet remained unassuming and unaware of her natural beauty.

Tracey and Jill were always together. They worked the same shift and floor at the center and could not wait to share rest and relaxation they knew was in store for them on this vacation. They talked incessantly of the sun, beaches, food and fun that they planned to experience together. They were both badly in need of a vacation and expected this to be their trip of a lifetime. It wasn't hard for Jill to talk Tracey into taking the cruise.

After second shift one night, we all stopped in to our favorite hangout, Dugan's, for a drink together before heading for home. With a job like the one we had, we often found ourselves needing to vent about the day and wind our nerves down a bit. We all served as Correction Officers and by then, I held the rank of Sergeant. Tracey and Jill were Corporals, and the fourth in our group, Joan, did not hold any rank.

Joan often served as our comic relief. We all loved her but she was quite the character. You might say Joan was a female Barney Fife. She was a walking skeleton, weighing less than 100 pounds. Ironically, she had exceptionally large breasts that she desperately tried to hide with several layers of shirts and sweaters. She often sported a baseball cap and was an avid sports fan. She could spout stats and team standings as well as any guy in the place. She was the youngest girl in a family of 7 boys. Her brothers taught her beer guzzling and belching skills that always helped to loosen her up and relax. Joan smoked like a chimney and was typically a nervous wreck at all times. She was not gay, but was assumed so by most who met her.

It was after a couple of beers that night, Jill got the idea that Joan and I should join her and Tracey on the cruise. It would be even more fun with four and she knew that we could use the vacation too. So, it was decided. The four of us would be taking the cruise together and we just could not wait to go.

Joan was paired up with me for the trip. She and I would be roommates. That was fine by Joan because she always looked to me for backup. I am what you might call a take charge personality. I guess that's why I was promoted to Sergeant. My size is an asset in this role. At six feet tall, I'm not your average female. Nothing about me is average. My shoe size is 12 and my bra size is 42H. I have the milk white skin of a fair Irish lassie and piercing green eyes. I guess you could say I am fairly fit but certainly not agile. I am also single at the age of 31. I am known as a guarded, protective, strong, officer. "Back to the wall" stern and strictly by the book. Although reserved and on the quiet side, you don't mess with Maggie Flannery and people pick up on that pretty quickly. I treated my team fairly and the same went for the inmates I was in charge of.

That makes up the crew of four who are going on the cruise together. You get to know each other pretty well when you are locked down together, guarding county inmates, and at threat for an uprising at any given moment. Boy did we ever need a vacation! The thought of a luxury cruise….the midnight buffets, the umbrella drinks on the beach, the cabana boys who will be at our beck and call. Oh yeah, I'm in all right. I am so in!

Chapter Four

Thursday night at the center. The second shift was taking its toll on me. I was feeling exhausted and not in the mood for any bullshit. But bullshit comes with this job. No escaping it. There is always somebody going off. Either faking a seizure so they can get some sick bay time and meds, or the typical altercation between two inmates who have gotten on each other's last nerve. Whatever it was, as Sergeant in charge of the shift, I had to be on the scene of any trouble.

Our county guests were a bit jumpy that night. Maybe excited because visitation the following day would bring loved ones in to see them, or maybe it was the full moon that was shining in the windows. In any case, I could feel it coming. The verge of some sort of catastrophe was all around me. You see I am known for having a sixth sense of sorts. I can tell when something is going to happen. Not just events either. Good or bad. I can look at a person and know if they are on the level or hiding a secret. I can spot trouble before it happens.

Inmates were all tucked in snug under their county issued grey flannel blankets. Those grey woolies, as we called them, must have felt pretty good that night because we got through the night without any issues. Amazing.

The next morning, however, was when all hell broke loose. The food line was progressing with no incident. The metal trays and cups with spoons were the standard issue for meal distribution. No forks or knives here. Hard wood tables with wooden benches allowed for orderly line-ups and clear observation. Everyone here was treated the same. No preferential treatment. Same 6:00 A.M. wake-up call, same food, same utensils, same seating. Funny thing was, the same held true for those of us in charge of the operation. No outside food was allowed to be brought into the center, so we had to eat the same food the inmates did, on the same trays, on the same benches. We were prisoners too. The difference was, we were paid to serve our time and they weren't.

The personalities you encounter in a job like mine were interesting to say the least. My fellow officers ranged from the military veterans who understood protocol and chain of command, to the wanna-be cops who failed to qualify for a police department role but nevertheless acted as though they had jurisdiction anywhere at all times. Then, of course, we had our share of screw-ups too. Rizzo comes to mind. He was 350 pounds of Italian goodness with the work ethic of a slug. Whenever there was trouble, he was always the last to arrive on scene. He moved at a snail's pace. On purpose. He would do anything to get out of working.

I was sitting at the control desk when the alarms went off and the emergency call came over the radio. When that happens, we all go running to the scene and we did. My intuition proves true again, as does the full moon effect. We have a situation.

Inmate #4646 was new to our facility. He obviously had never been jailed before. He was a little bit "slow" and had a hard time understanding and conforming to our procedures. That didn't prevent him from buying the heroin from an undercover agent on the street that got him locked up in here. He knew enough to shoot himself up. In any case, he landed here two nights ago and proved to be a pain in our ass immediately. Not because he was hostile, just because he was stupid. So stupid in fact that the moron puts his hand in the cell door as it was electronically closing. When those cell doors are on "close" mode, there is no stopping them. They don't stop because there is something in the way. They just keep closing. As they did when #4646 almost got his hand out of the way in time, but for the finger that was severed by the door. The alarm goes off and all doors are locked down.

The blood was gushing, and my team went into action. The medical team got a gurney to the scene very quickly and got #4646 strapped down and on his way to St. Vincent's hospital in less than 10 minutes. The EMT working the ambulance reconnoitered the situation. "Severed finger on the right hand of this thirty-five-year old, white male inmate. "Who's got the finger?" he asks. "The finger? Oh shit. Who's got the finger?" That's the question I get over the radio as we are trying to bring order back to the cell block where it happened. Most of the action is over, and who was just now arriving on the scene? Rizzo. Of course. Typical Rizzo. Hoping that everything is taken care of and over by the time he gets to the scene. Taking his good old time. Well this time, he's getting the finger, literally!

"Who's still at the scene of the accident?" I scream into the radio. "Arriving at the cell now Sarge." "This is Rizzo." "Rizzo....do you see the finger? You have to find the finger." "Rizzo, do you see the finger?"

"10-4 Sarge. I see the finger. What the hell am I supposed to do with it?"

"Rizzo pick up the finger and wrap it up in your shirt tail. Get to the garage and take a Sheriff's car to St. Vincent's Emergency room as quickly as you can. Use the lights and siren and get that finger there pronto."

"Oh Sarge, are you messin with me? I really have to do that?"

"You'll do it and you'll do it now, or I'll have your ass fired." "That's what you get for arriving last to the scene." "This time it bit you in the ass."

Back at the desk when all the commotion was over, we laughed our asses off about Rizzo. Served him right! We could usually find the humor in any situation once the immediate danger was over. That's what kept us all close. We looked out for each other.

I can still remember my first week at the center. My eyes were so wide and my innocent view of the world came crashing down pretty quickly. During roll call on day one, there were twelve of us that were newly hired as CO's. We got little to no training, but were instructed to always call inmates by their given name. Whatever is on the record as their name is what we were supposed to call them.

I was very new on the job and working that second shift that I always seemed to be stuck on. I was assigned to stand guard over a female pod. One guard, me, and 24 inmates. I really didn't like those odds but that was the reality of the position I was in. I wasn't sure why, but female inmates were given the privilege of wearing their own bathrobe and slippers at night. The men were not so lucky. They had to stay in their jail issued uniforms at all times. I was never fond of the color orange, but this job gave me a whole new distain for that color.

It was a very cold winter night, and the center was famous for keeping the temperature chilly, just on the verge of cold. All the females were walking around in their personal robes and slippers, trying to stay warm. I found it necessary to address one of them for bothering another inmate. She had her back to me and I'd never seen her before. This was her first night in the pod. I did know her name was Carolyn.

"Hey Carolyn" I yelled. This creature immediately turned around to look me up and down and fiercely stated with the most booming voice I'd ever heard, "My name is Howard!" "Oh", I said, "Okay Howard, back off that inmate or you'll be facing solitary." Fortunately he/she did as told because I needed to tuck myself away for a minute to gain my composure back. You see, that was my first exposure to a person in "transition" and I have to admit it was a bit shocking for me.

This job caused me to grow up....and fast! I saw, heard, and experienced things I never dreamed of as an innocent, Irish Catholic girl civilian. I was born second in a string of five kids in the Flannery family. My mom had four girls before my brother, Prince Edward, was born. Took five tries, but my dad finally got his son. Ed was the favored child. He got his own bedroom. One of the three in our little west side bungalow. Of course mom and dad had a bedroom, so that left one more for me and my three sisters to share. Talk about cramped and crowded. Two double beds jammed together in that room. Ann got Rose as her bed mate and I shared a double with my sister Patty. Both my mom and dad were of Irish heritage, so you could not get more Irish than Maggie Flannery. 100% Irish, no hiding it. It came with the quick temper, extreme guilt, and devoted work ethic that runs in our family, as well as a quick wit and keen sense of humor. Good thing too. I could not do this job without a sense of humor.

Dad was a blue collar worker, doing his time at the local steel mill. Mom held the household together, doing the usual cooking, cleaning, and keeping the kids under control. And oh yeah, she also baked. She baked bread, pies, biscuits, coffee cakes, cookies and birthday cakes for every birthday that came up during the year. In our family, that was a lot of birthdays. Five kids, Dad, Mom, and Grandma who moved in with us when I was about twelve. Not that we had room for her. We really didn't. But mom and dad converted our dining room into a first floor bedroom for Gran. They had a half bath built so she had her very own facilities. And God help you if you tried to use it. Oh no. That was off limits to us. We were not allowed to use Gran's bathroom. If we had to go, we had to go upstairs. No exceptions. We all loved Gran. She was a real character. Irish to the bone. She was also hard of hearing, so we all got in the habit of yelling at her at the top of our lungs just to have a conversation. Add that to the craziness of the Flannery household and you get the picture of how it was for me growing up. It was all pretty wild, but definitely made me the woman I am today. You learn to hold your own when you're fighting for the last pork chop at the dinner table.

Chapter Five

It was 2:00 A.M... February in Cleveland is ugly. The rain did not let up and added to the pain of the bone chilling cold and the treacherous icy roads. The crash site was dark. It was a residential street with no streetlights. Sort of a country road. By now, we were all at the scene and could not believe our eyes.

The car actually hydroplaned in a large puddle and went straight with the full-force of 60 mph into a tree. They were going too fast, especially in these conditions. They were in a hurry to get back to the house to get to sleep for our 10:00 A.M. flight the next morning. We thought staying all together at Tracey's house on the eve of our big trip would be smart. We never dreamed anything like this could happen.

Tracey took the worst of the crash. As the driver, and not wearing a seatbelt, she hit the dashboard before she went through the windshield. Her face was severely cut, bruised and already swollen twice its normal size. Her front teeth were gone. Her foot was crushed and caught under the dashboard. She was unconscious and non-responsive. The first-responders were working diligently to free her from the wreckage and get her in the waiting ambulance. That was the first time I ever saw the "jaws of life" in action. It literally pealed that car door open and they were able to pull the dashboard off her.

Jill was also unconscious at first but came to when the EMT called her name. It was obvious that her arms were broken, and she was badly bruised all over.

They were both on the way to the hospital and we were right behind them. Crews went to work immediately on them and the rest of us paced the waiting room with vending machine coffee. The coffee was just as bitter as the situation we faced.

As horrible as it was for Tracey and Jill, Joan and I looked at each other and said simultaneously, "What are we going to do now?" They obviously were not going to make the cruise vacation. In their situation, the travel agency would allow for a refund. Joan and I were obligated to the trip and we would not receive a refund if we cancelled.

"OK Joan. Let's talk about this. What ARE we going to do? If we don't show up for this cruise trip tomorrow, we'll be out $1,000."

"There is no way I would feel right about going now. I feel just awful. I'm sick about this. You do what you want Maggie, but I'm not going. I don't care about the money."

"Are you sure? You absolutely will not go?" "You're going to lose all that money and no vacation."

"I just can't do it Maggie. I'm not going….in fact I'm going home right now."

I sat there stunned. Is this really happening? Do I really have to take this cruise by myself? Oh no…. I had a better idea.

Chapter Six

It was 4:00 A.M... "Rose. Wake up. Wake up, Rose."

"Why, what's going on?"

"You're going on the cruise with me."

"What are you talking about, leave me alone, I'm sleeping."

"No you're not. Get up right now."

"Will you please leave me alone, I have to go to work in the morning." "No, you are going on vacation with me."

That was enough to get Rose up. "What happened?" "What are you talking about?" "There was a horrible accident. Tracey and Jill are both in the hospital. Their car hit a tree and they are both really messed up." "There's nothing I can do for them at this point, so I still want to take the trip." "Joan won't go with me and I don't want to go alone. So you have to come with me."

"Are you crazy? I just started my job last week. I can't get any time off to go on vacation. There's no way." "I'll call your boss. I know her pretty well. I'll explain what happened and see if she can give you the time off. It's worth a shot. Otherwise I have to go on the cruise by myself. I really don't want to have to do that Rose. PLEASE! Let me call her and see what she says." "The office isn't even open till eight. That's four hours from now."

"OK, I know. In the meantime let's get you packed and ready to go. Move it, the plane leaves at 10. Rose was still half asleep and very confused. I went into action. She's coming with me come hell or high water.

My sister Rose is four years younger than me. Chronologically that is. If you measured her naiveté, inexperience, and trusting nature, you would size her up to be about 16. She is really a sweetheart but too much of a trusting soul. Her looks make up for any of her shortfalls. She is the cutest thing ever. She's got the biggest, bluest eyes, and a figure that always catches the eyes of any guy she passes. She's what my mom called "a real looker." I love her unconditionally and have always looked out for her. I always did what I could to shield and protect her from harm and the ugliness the world can offer. Rose depended on me to some extent as her sister, her roommate, and her protector. I would do anything for her and watch out if you ever tried to hurt her or take advantage of her. You would have me to deal with me!

She had no idea, at the moment, what she was in store for. At that rate, neither did I.

Chapter Seven

I found another suitcase in the basement and brought it up to Rose's room. I started throwing underwear and t-shirts in it while Rose was in the shower. Where are all her summer clothes? All I see in her dresser is long sleeve shirts and jeans. She must have stored her summer clothes in the basement. Back down I go. Jackpot....I found the right box and pulled out a few pairs of shorts, a bathing suit, and some tank tops.

I'm throwing all this in the suitcase while it occurs to me that I have to get the ticket changed over from Joan's name to Rose's name. I told Joan I would pay her for the ticket if I could get it transferred to Rose. She was counting on that! How am I going to pull this off?

I called my other sister Patty. Patty was the business woman in the family who had a lot of experience. She'll know how to handle this. She can help us here. By now it's 6:00 A.M. Patty please answer, please answer the phone. "Hello." "Patty it's Maggie." "What's wrong?" "It's a long story. Jill and Tracey were in a bad accident last night. Their car hit a tree." "Oh my god. Are they OK?" "Well, they are both severely injured, but they're not going to die or anything." "Thank God for that." "I know, but now the vacation is all screwed up. They can't go and Joan refuses to go without them." "OK but why are you calling me about this?"

"You have to help me Patty. I am going to bring Rose on the trip, but we need to get Joan's tickets transferred into Rose's name. Can you call the travel agency and see if you can get this done? PLEASE Patty. I really need your help right now. While you do that, I'm going to call Rose's boss and see if I can get her a week's vacation." "Didn't she just start that job last week? How are you going to do that?" "I'm not sure. Wish me luck. I'm going to call Mary right now and see what I can do. I know her pretty well from seeing her at county political functions. I have a feeling she'll help me out on this. "

Its 8:01 and I'm on the phone with Rose's boss, Mary Cooney, the County Clerk of Courts. "Good morning Mary. This is Maggie Flannery." "Oh, hi Maggie. What can I do for you?" "Well Mary, this is a pretty wild request, and I do apologize." What, what is it?" "It's kind of a long story. Two of my friends are in critical condition from an accident last night." "Oh that's awful." "I know, but here's the thing." They were supposed to be leaving with me today on a cruise vacation. Now I have no one to go with." "Okay?" "Well, I'm calling to ask you if you could somehow grant my sister Rose a week's vacation. She just started working in your department last Monday." "Oh I see." "Well I could process approval for advance time off but she won't have any other vacation time coming until next year."

"That's fine Mary. I'm sure she'll be good with that." "Okay, consider this a favor on behalf of our longstanding friendship. I would not do this for just anybody you know." "I know Mary. I cannot tell you how much I appreciate your help. Thank you so much."

Rose is not going to believe this. I can hardly believe it myself. Alright, that's the first step in pulling this off.

I just hang up and the phone rings. Patty is calling to tell me she found an emergency number for the travel agency. She somehow worked a miracle and got everything transferred into Rose's name. The flights and the cruise ticket. We were in business!

The next hurdle is finding a legitimate ID for Rose. You see, she doesn't drive, so she has no driver's license, nor passport. She was so new on the job; she didn't even have her work picture ID yet. God only knows where her birth certificate was. Next I call my mom, who, by the way, lived downstairs from me and Rose with our Dad. It was her and my dad's house that we were renting the upstairs of.

"Mom, it's Maggie." "What's going on up there? It sounds like you two are running laps." "Mom, do you know where Rose's birth certificate is?" "No. Not really." "Why?" "Mom, it's a long story I don't have time to get into right now. Just please help me find Rose's birth certificate. She's coming on the cruise with me and she needs an ID to leave the country." "Oh really?" "OK, let me go see if I can find it." "I'll bring it up if I can."

Rose is downing a bowl of Kix while I am calling a cab for a ride to the airport. I hear Mom coming up the back stairs. Thank God. She's found it. "Well, I can't find the birth certificate, but I found this." "What's that?" "Her baptismal certifi-

27

cate." "It shows her birth date right here." "And it's signed by Monsignor Murphy." "That should be good enough to prove her citizenship, don't you think"? "Not only is she a US citizen, she's also a good Catholic!" "Surely this will work!"

"I don't know Mom, but it will have to do. The cab is outside, and we have to go. "OK, well be careful and have a good time." "We will mom. Thanks for your help."

Rose was still in shock. Not quite sure what was happening, but we were in the cab and on our way to the airport. Vacation, here we come!!

Chapter Eight

I couldn't believe it. We were actually on the plane on our way to Miami. From there we would have to take a much smaller plane into Antigua. The travel agent explained that the ship was not large enough to dock at any of the larger ports and that's why we would be boarding in Antigua. I thought that was a bit strange. A cruise ship too small to dock in the port of Miami? Oh well, I wasn't going to worry about it. We were on our way and that was all I cared about. Soon we would be boarding The Phantom. That was the name of our cruise ship. For now, I really wish I could enjoy a well-earned snooze. The craziness of the morning and the night before really wore me out. I just can't sleep on planes. I always feel like I am stuffed in a sardine can. There is just no way to get comfortable. Rose on the other hand conked out in a matter of seconds. So I have no one to talk to during this flight. I decided to pour over the travel brochure again and make sure we weren't missing any important details. I sat there day dreaming about the upcoming week and couldn't wait to get there.

Rose woke up to the captain's announcement that we were about to arrive in Miami. We had to pick up our luggage from baggage claim because we had to go through Customs to board our next flight to Antigua. Unfortunately, we had an extended lay-over. It was around two o'clock in the afternoon by the time we got through Customs, and our Antigua flight did not leave until 6:30 P.M. Four and a half hours to burn. We weren't comfortable enough to leave the airport, so we found a spot to grab some food and tried to relax.

Rose was finally starting to grasp what was happening. She couldn't believe we were sitting at the Miami airport, waiting to board our plane to Antigua. We both had a good laugh about the 4:00 A.M. wake-up call and all that went on to get us to this point. Here she was, on vacation, after only one week on the job. That's going to go over well with her new co-workers!

My mind went to thinking of Tracey and Jill and hoping they were alright. I'd hope they would understand that my going ahead with the vacation did not mean I wasn't concerned for them. Surely they could understand and would do the same if they found themselves in this situation. I would have called them both at this point, but you see, in 1986, I didn't own a cell phone. They weren't too abundant in those early days of mobile phone technology. It was 1983 that Motorola released the first commercial mobile phone at the cost of almost $4000. I certainly could not afford to own a mobile phone, and that was the case for all of my friends as well.

I really didn't want to go through the hassle of making two long distance calls at a pay phone, so instead I just said a couple Hail Mary's for them and asked the Lord to look out for them.

That would have to do. I'll be sure and pick up some souvenirs to bring them when I get back home. Hopefully they will be out of the hospital by then.

Before long we heard a boarding announcement for our flight to Antigua. Time to hustle back to the gate. The plane we saw out the window of the airport was so small; it could not even pull into the gate. We had to go outside, walk along a marked path, and walk up a portable staircase into the prop plane. The plane held about 20 people. We assumed most everyone boarding that plane was going on the same cruise we were, because the passengers were giddy with excitement. I heard the woman behind us mention shoeless cruise. My ears perked up. I turned around to ask her if she might be going on the Phantom cruise. Turns out she was. I guessed her age around 30 and she was thin, fit, and beautiful. She went on to share her lifelong wish to go on a shoeless cruise and she was over the moon at this point. I noticed the emblem on her jacket pocket. It looked like something to do with sailing so I asked her about it. "Oh yes." "I'm a member of the Erie Sail club. I don't own a sailboat, but I crew on one. I do have a bit of experience crewing, but this cruise, no doubt, will really challenge my skills." "I've been waiting for this opportunity for an ocean sail." "That will put me in a whole new skill level at the club".

"Well that's nice." "I guess I'll see you when we land then."

"Rose, what do you think she's talking about? Crewing? Maybe she has some kind of special ticket or something." "I have no idea, but I'm going to try and get some sleep so please don't bother me. OK?" "I wish I could sleep on a plane. I'm exhausted."

But no luck there. Excitement or nerves, there was no way I could relax enough to fall asleep. The job I had turned me into a suspicious personality. I trusted no one and I was always on the lookout for trouble. I wished that just this once I could relax and have a good time. Maybe Rose's attitude would rub off on me. I could only hope.

Three and a half hours later, we are getting set to land. By now it was dark. Pitch black dark. Out the window we see a short strip of blue lights and nothing else. Our landing was a bit rough to say the least. I was glad to be on the ground. We heard an announcement with instructions on exiting the plane and entering the hanger. Hanger? Really? The portable staircase was once again rolled up to the door and we began exiting the plane. The only thing in sight was an open-air hanger. We were told to head that direction. I literally had to hold Rose's shoulder to help me navigate toward the light. It was so dark, I couldn't see where I was walking, and I was afraid to move. We had to walk a hundred yards or so to the hanger where we were told to claim our luggage.

We got to the building and saw a group of locals waiting around and talking to each other. It sounded like English but with a Caribbean twist. Maybe Antiguan Creole English. In any case, they were very hard to understand. Rose and I spot our bags. We gather them up and set them on the portable card table serving as a luggage counter. As we are fidgeting with our purses to retrieve our transportation information, our bags get pushed to the end of the table where the locals are standing. One of them grabs them both and takes off running. He's out of the hanger in a matter of seconds and our bags are gone with him. Damn it. "Come on Rose. We have to go after him and get our bags back." We were not even out of the airport and trouble had found us already. So here we go, running like two fools, chasing this native in the dark who had our luggage. He had the jump on us and ran way faster than we did. There was just no way we were going to catch him. Great! Just great!

He suddenly stops running. He's now standing in front of an ancient Volkswagen Beetle Bug stuffing our bags into the trunk. Which by the way, is in the front of the car. He looks up at us and says, "Ten dollars ship." Rose and I look at each other and get in the car. Now you have to remember that here I am 6' tall and not exactly thin. Rose is slightly shorter than me, but a whole lot thinner. The front seat is pushed back as far as it goes and our knees are in our mouth. Hopefully this ride won't be too long. I felt paralyzed after five minutes in that squeeze box and wasn't sure I would be able to walk again once we got out. The smell inside that cab was horrible. I wasn't sure what was worse. The drivers dime store cologne, or the aroma of left-over lunches and cigarettes he had piled up between his and his passenger seat. The back seats we were sitting on were ripped up with moldy yellow stuffing sticking out. The floor was filthy, and our heads were brushing up against the ceiling of the cab where we see spider webs and what looks like some kind of matted up fur. Oh Lord, I thought the plane was bad. Our driver is heading down a dirt road that he must have navigated frequently because it was so dark, we couldn't see a thing. We weren't sure how he spotted the cow that decided to cross our path on the road, but he did and we were stopped to let it pass by us. We could see it in the headlights of the car as it meandered past. Needless to say we were terrified and not feeling too sure that we would ever see the ship.

The car continued on the road for a short distance and it stopped again. Holy Mother of God. What now?

Another man gets into the car. He's wearing dirty clothes, muddy boots, and has a bandana tied around his long greasy hair. He's talking to the driver in a foreign language we don't understand. They are laughing together. We don't see anything funny! We start down the road again and I am absolutely sure we are in trouble. I whispered to Rose, "Get ready. We are going to have to fight these guys off us." Rose looked at me like I had two heads. She wasn't catching my drift immediately, but when I showed her my fist, she got the idea pretty quickly. I was pretty sure I could take the driver out. After all he was about 5'6" and all of 150 pounds. His friend wasn't much bigger and I figured Rose could handle him. I see the driver eyeing me in the rear-view mirror. He's checking us out and I don't like it. I took my keys and fashioned my own set of brass knuckles by putting a key between each finger and making a fist. I was ready. These guys won't know what hit them. Rose is looking at me terrified. The car stops again. OK....this is it. I was ready for a fight.

The driver got out of the car and started taking our bags out of the trunk. The other guy pushes back the front seat and motions for us to get out. "Ten dollars!" We are in the middle of nowhere. It's pitch black, there is nothing and no one to be seen. I said "Ship?" As his partner finishes up throwing our bags out onto the dirt road, he points to a hill. He says "Ship."

I gave him the ten dollars and the two of them drove off leaving us stranded. We felt lucky to get out of that car alive.

We figured the worst was behind us now and soon we would be on that ship enjoying our luxurious vacation. All we had to do now was find it.

Chapter Nine

We are absolutely spent. Totally exhausted. Riding on planes all day, and not sleeping a wink the night before, I wasn't sure I was going to be able to carry my suitcase much less start walking. I didn't want Rose to know my feelings and concern, so I mustered up the strength to pick up my bag as Rose picked up hers. At least we weren't harmed. We can do this...

Rose and I started walking. We are heading to the hill that the driver pointed out to us. We were literally feeling our way down the road when we saw the slightest crack of light. As we kept walking toward it I was praying to God that this wasn't THAT light and that we weren't really dead.

The hill might as well have been Mount Everest. We were struggling to keep going up, up and up. Our bags were getting heavier with every step. Mother of God, somebody help us.

Just as we were getting to the top of the hill, we saw what looked like the top of a fence. We kept going. Yes, it was a fence all right, with a razor wire top. An open field was before us surrounded by this razor wire fence. I felt for a moment that I was back in the center recreation yard. What was going on?

As we got to the very top of the hill, we could see it on the horizon. It appeared like a silhouette against the black night. It was a pirate ship. No lie. I was waiting for Captain Hook to come out at any minute. A wooden pirate ship. "Oh my God Rose." "It's a ghost ship." The closer we walked toward the ship, the worse it looked. I could see ripped up sails on the masts blowing in the wind. The bow was covered in barnacles and the portals were all cracked and shattered.

We made it to the pier where the ship was docked. There was no one in sight and we weren't sure what to do. We sat on our bags, trying to catch our breath and get our thoughts together. "Hey girlies." "Come on up the plank so we can check you in." "You going on the shoeless cruise?" "Do we have a choice?"

We literally had to walk a wooden plank that was about two feet wide, bags in tow, to board the ship. We made it. We did not see any other passengers. Was everybody else already on board? We were welcomed on board by a skinny islander who pointed us toward the "dining room." "Sign in. Sign in." We signed the passenger log book. We spotted a "welcome" table. It featured a luxurious pitcher of water, without ice, and a stack of paper cups. The kind you use in your bathroom that are about two inches high. We were so desperate for a drink of anything we were happy to see it.

After our refreshing welcome treat, we were directed down a hallway. "You room 666." Oh great. As if we haven't been cursed enough already, now we are being sent to the devils den. Room 666 – perfect. The bag drag wasn't over yet. There was no one there to help carry our bags, so we proceeded to pick them up and head to room 666. Following the cardboard signs in the hallway, we saw that room 666 was evidently downstairs. I use that word loosely. There was a rickety wooden ladder that was literally straight up and down. No lean whatsoever. I made Rose go first while I stayed on the upper deck with the bags. Somehow, some way, she got down the ladder and was standing on the lower deck. OK great. I said, "Watch out," and threw our bags down the hole one at a time. Rose was able to catch them but it just about knocked her over. My turn. I had about a half-inch clearance on either side of the ladder. My double H girls took the worst of it, but I made it. Onward to room 666.

As my protective big sister instinct kicked in, I opened the door first. I thought it best I check it out for a second before Rose came in. "Step in will ya?" "I am in." Our cabin was the size of a slightly larger than average closet. We did not see any place to put our bags, so we had to throw them up on the bunk beds. There was barely enough clearance between the top and lower bunk to fit the suitcase. It was about a three foot space between bunks. There was about a two foot clearance between the upper bunk and the ceiling. Since I was older, and quite a bit bigger than Rose, I begged her to take the upper bunk. Thankfully she agreed.

Since we were both in the cabin, I thought it best to lock the door. Well that wasn't going to happen. The lock on the door was broke. There was no way to lock our door. Perfect. Now we're going to have to take our passports, money, and credit cards with us wherever we go. "Good thing I packed two fanny packs."

"And speaking of packing, what the hell did you pack in my suitcase? Is this really the best you could do?" "I've got five tee shirts, two pairs of shorts, a skirt, a blouse, one sundress, and one nightgown." "No extra bra, one swimsuit, and 5 pair of underpants." "I'm not going to make a very good impression on our fellow passengers with this wardrobe." "What if Mr. Right is on board?" "So what if he is." "Maybe he'll take pity on you as a poor, innocent, Catholic girl and fall madly in love with you." "Yeah right." "We're going to have to go shopping at the first port we land at." "I can't live with this rag tag collection of vacation wear." "So plan on shopping, okay?" "Yeah, yeah, let's worry about that tomorrow. Right now, we have to get organized."

We saw a closed door in the room and assumed it was our bathroom. "Let's check that out." We opened the door and saw a toilet. I stepped inside the cubby of a room. I could not extend my arms without hitting the wall on either side. It had to be only two feet in diameter. I looked up at the ceiling and saw a showerhead right over the toilet. What a timesaver. How convenient. We could go to the toilet and take a shower at the same time. It didn't even have a shower curtain. There was a tiny sink, no vanity. A shallow shelf ran around the perimeter of the bathroom with a small ridge at the edge. We supposed that was to keep your toiletries and such from falling off the shelf. The water in the toilet was shall we say "recycled." It was obviously not fresh. There was a "shower instruction" card placed strategically on the toilet top. Better read that.

The shower had a button that needed to be held in for the water to come out. If you let up pressure on the button, the water would stop. The instructions demanded that you commence your shower by holding in the shower button long enough to get wet. Then you must release the button while you soap up. Once washed, you were to depress the button again to rinse off. Now I've heard of water conservation before, but this was a bit drastic. It was obviously an issue on the ship.

Our vacation adventure had the beginnings of a disaster. We were both so exhausted that night, we just wanted to go to bed. I went first in the shower. I placed my toiletries in the sink while taking a quick shower. That kept them in easy reach. As I rinsed the conditioner out of my hair, I pushed the button again to get wet so I could soap up and wash off the grime of the day. As I go to depress the button, I drop the bar of soap. Wonderful. I bend over to pick up the soap and my ass hits the bathroom door. It opens, and there I am, naked and afraid. Exposed to Rose who is hysterically laughing at me. I can't take much more. I swear, I'm going to lose it. I just want to get some sleep. As I finished up, I placed all my soap, lotions, shampoo, conditioners, and perfume on the perimeter shelf. It was Rose's turn. She had a bit of an easier time, only because she fit in the bathroom better than I did. Her ass was not going to bump the door open on her.

The moment of truth. Am I going to fit in this bunk bed? Looking at the bunks, I could not believe my eyes. The grey woolies. The same grey blankets that are used at the correction center are on these bunks. They were tucked in so tight on the bunks that we had to undo the beds just to get in. This is a nightmare. Maybe I'm already sleeping. God I hope so.

We were finally in bed. As best as I could fit. My feet hung off the end by at least a foot, and I overlapped the width of the bunk just enough to make it uncomfortable. We could feel that the ship was departing the port. The ocean waves were going to play havoc with this tug. It was then I realized that the grey woolies were tucked in so tight to literally hold you in the bunk. I was starting to drift off when I heard plunk, plunk, plunk. "Rose! You did close the lid of the toilet as I asked you to when you finished your shower, didn't you?" No response. She was already out. I got up to check. Sure enough, all my toiletries had fallen off the shelf and right into the toilet, including my toothbrush and toothpaste. Of course, Rose decided to keep all her stuff in her little ditty bag. Her things were all safe and sound, still on top of her suitcase, which by the way, we had to stack on top of the one wooden bench that was in our cabin. I retrieved all my toiletries, no pun intended, and proceeded to wash them off in an effort to salvage what I could.

I wedged myself back into the bunk. I was so tired by now I was almost crying. So close to drifting off when our cabin lights came on. What now? Is this some kind of a drill? Rose woke up. Just as I was about to get up and see what it was all about, the lights went off again. On, off. On, off. I knew it. We did get the haunted cabin. Rose was totally freaking out. I was just livid. This went on for about fifteen minutes before I figured out what was happening. I had hung some bags on a hook over the light switch. As the ship rocked back, and forth, so did the bags across the light switch. Every time the ship swung left, the lights went on. Then when it swung back to the right, the lights went off. If we weren't so exhausted we may have found this to be funny. At the time, we were just overcome with exhaustion and totally aggravated. I got up and moved the bags off the hook. Finally sleep…

Chapter Ten

It must be morning. We did not have a portal in our cabin, so we couldn't tell if the sun was up or not. But we were both awake and feeling hungry. The one instruction we remembered being given when we checked in on the ship was that we were to remain barefoot for the length of the cruise. It was very important that we do so. We were also told to go to the dining room area when we heard the ships bell. The bell was ringing and we were starving. We had to get dressed one at a time because we did not fit together if we tried to do it simultaneously. I went first. "You know what Rose?" "I don't care what everybody else does, I'm going to leave my shoes on. I just don't feel comfortable being barefoot." "Everyone will see my feet." Rose agreed. After all, I found this really cute pair of red sandals at Wal-Mart that were perfect for the outfit I was going to wear. I wasn't going to miss the opportunity to make my debut a stylish one. We both kept our shoes on and headed up the ladder to find our way to the dining room. We had to step over the doorway to enter the dining room. Right at that moment, the ship must have been hit by a huge wave and it shifted to the right. As we made our entrance into the dining room we found the floor to be like an ice skating rink. We reluctantly turned into a sister act doing the Soul Train dance. I was the first to hit the table and Rose was right behind me attached to my backside. We landed with arms stretched out and bent over from the waist right onto the table. I looked at the passengers seated at the table and said, "I guess we'll sit here." We took our places on the wooden bench, at the wooden table and tried to appear poised and sociable. After all, this was our first opportunity to meet fellow passengers. After that entrance, we knew we'd be remembered.

The placemats on the table were soaking wet. There were wet rags under the creamers and sugar bowls. This was so that they would not slide off the table. We skated our way to the buffet line. There they were, the metal trays and cups we used every day in the jail. We worked our way through the line like a couple of prisoners that we were. There was no silverware to be found. It was not allowed. This meal would be hand held.

An island woman ran the kitchen. She could be described as a witch doctor, a voodoo princess, or as I liked to call her, the kitchen witch. She was five feet tall and four feet wide. She barked orders like the jail warden. She proceeded to fill us in on the rules of the dining room. I was all about rules, and could relate to her need to control the crowd of passengers. We were instructed to eat what was served and don't ask for seconds. Guess there's no midnight buffet on this cruise. Between meals you could have a cold drink without ice, or a lukewarm cup of coffee. Both drinks were the same temperature.

Breakfast consisted of some type of egg sandwich with an undefined piece of meat in it and a slice of cheese. It was portable and could be eaten without utensils. We got a Dixie cup of orange juice and one cup of the lukewarm coffee. It was barely edible, but we devoured the sandwich like it was filet mignon. The guy sitting next to me went back in line to get a second sandwich. I was about to take his lead when the kitchen witch started screaming. "I told you no seconds. Everybody gets the same thing. One sandwich. Go sit down, no more food for you." Unbelievable!

Since we had our limit for breakfast, we were about to skate our way back to our cabin when the ship gong went off announcing a lifeboat drill. All passengers were told to go back to their cabins, put on their lifejackets and return to the deck for instructions. This was going to be interesting. We made it back to the cabin safely and proceeded to put on our lifejackets. Of course, Rose had no issue, and got it on with no problem. I was another story. That vest was not going to fit around my double H girls. No way. I tried everything. I loosened every strap to the max. I pushed, pulled, and twisted. Nothing worked. I had to go to the deck with the vest still open and ask for an extender. That turned out to be a small piece of rope. Once again, I am a standout. Embarrassed as I was, I decided to stay low profile in the back of the crowd.

"Women and children upfront." "All women and children upfront." "You, lady with the rope." "Get up here. You have to get in front." So much for staying low profile.

As part of the lifeboat drill, the captain proceeds to warn us about a danger on the beaches. It seems there is a thorny creature of some sort that lives in the sand. Stepping on one would cause a thorn to enter your foot with an extremely painful result. These thorns are virtually impossible to pull out of your foot without doing a lot of damage. The only way to relieve the situation is to urinate on the spot where the thorn entered. We'd never heard of such a thing, but we definitely took notes on that one.

One of the crew was walking toward us and stopped next to Rose. He was obviously attracted to her. "Don't you worry honey. If you get a thorn, I will pee on your foot. It would be my pleasure." "Okay, thanks. Good to know."

Rose was not comfortable around this guy. We didn't know his name, so we started calling him Pee Wee. We started noticing that Pee Wee always seemed to be around us. Wherever we went on board, he was nearby. He definitely had the hots for Rose. She wasn't having any of it, and started trying to avoid him. That effort seemed near impossible on board, so we decided to go on the day's excursion trip. The itinerary for the day included beach time, lunch on shore, and some shopping time. It all sounded good to us. We were anchored off the island of St. Kitts. The island had no dock so it was necessary to use small motorized tender boats to get to the island. I sensed adventure ahead.

Chapter Eleven

The correct way to disembark the ship would have been from the port side of the boat. Well that was a problem because the stairs on the port side were rusted away and not usable. This meant we had to use the starboard side of the ship. The waves were very rough on the starboard side and were causing the small tender boats to bounce up and down a lot. The procedure for getting from the ship to the shore boat was supposedly very simple. You stand at the top of the stairs and wait until you were told to step off. There were two crewmen on either side of the stairs to assist. I estimated they weighed about 200 pounds. Together. This is going to be interesting. The problem was, both the tender boat and the ship were bouncing up and down with the waves. The plan was to wait until both boats were on the same bounce and then step off the stairs and onto the tender boat. The two crew members would hold you by the arms until you were safely onboard the tender boat. I was feeling very nervous and uneasy about this situation. I am not the most coordinated person and I knew I would not be exactly easy to hold up if need be. I asked Rose to go first so I could watch the procedure work. Of course she had no issue and it all went very smoothly. She was on board the tender boat in a matter of seconds.

Now it's my turn. I stepped up to the stairs and the two crewmen took my arms. I waited for them to give me the order to step out. Just as they did, the boat dropped about three to four feet on a wave. I swung out like an overweight Peter Pan and they literally dropped me into the boat the moment it came back up. I plopped down right in the aisle between everyone who had already boarded. The crew members had nerve enough to tell me to get up, sit down, and make room for others. I was totally mortified. Again.

We eventually made it to shore and I tried to put the whole ugly scene out of my head. We were going to enjoy this day if it killed me. The island was breathtakingly beautiful. I'd never seen such big, colorful, flowering trees. However, it was 90 degrees in the shade, but the problem was there was no shade to be found. The sun was unrelenting and we were melting as we walked among the straw market shopping. I was never one to do well in the heat and I was starting to feel sick. We spotted a bench on the street and made a beeline for it. At least we were able to sit for a bit, even if it was in the sun. We were so thirsty, my lips were stuck together. I was sweating bullets and I badly needed something to drink.

As if sent from heaven, I see this island boy riding up to us on his bicycle with an empty bottle of Pepsi. "Pepsi?" he asked. "Yes, yes, for sure. We would like a Pepsi. How much?" "Ten dollar" he said. OK. Relief is in store, even if it is outrageously priced. I didn't care at that point. I got a twenty dollar bill out of my fanny pack and asked him to bring us two Pepsi's. "Sure thing" he said as he rode away with the twenty. We sat there melting in the sun for thirty minutes waiting for him before we finally admitted to ourselves that we were taken for a ride on that bicycle and it did not include getting any Pepsi.

By now it's lunch time, so we head to the designated gathering point to get lunch from the ship. The kitchen crew arrives with a basket of sandwiches and a basket of apples. One sandwich and one apple. That was our ration for lunch. Fortunately, they did have jugs of water also, so we were able to fill up our Dixie cup for a drink. As we ate our lunch, I noticed a lot of islanders gathering around the fringes of our picnic spot. Most passengers ate and left to continue shopping, but my radar was going off and I decided to stick around to see what was going down there.

A short distance from where we ate, I saw the kitchen witch collecting money from the locals who were buying our lunch leftovers. They were actually standing in a line as if this was a practice they were quite familiar with. This really set me off. Here we were, being rationed to one sandwich as full paying passengers on this "cruise line", and the food we paid for is being sold for the benefit of the kitchen witch. It wasn't right, and I was fuming. I wasn't quite sure what I was going to do about it, but I would deal with it later.

Rose and I decided to check out the beach. We had our bathing suits on under our clothes. Probably why we were so hot. We found an open spot with a couple of low sand chairs so we grabbed it. The water was absolutely beautiful. It was hard to tell where the sky ended and the water started. Now it was starting to feel like we were on vacation. If there is one thing that I love about vacation, it's sitting on the beach and watching the waves ebb back and forth. It was so peaceful and soothing. I felt myself actually relaxing. Well, that didn't last long.

We couldn't have been sitting on the beach for more than ten minutes when we heard the screaming. One of the ship's passengers was running on the beach without foot protection and stepped on one of those thorny creatures. He was screaming in pain as others started to gather around him. We knew what was coming. The poor guy was begging other guys to pee on his foot. One by one the guys relieved themselves on him with a stream of urine. I'm not sure how many guys it took for the thorn to come out, but we were not about to stick around to find out. We decided to head back to the ship early with our shoes on. We'd had enough of St. Kitts.

We made our way back to the little motor boat and got on with no incident. Amazing! Also in the boat was an older couple. I would guess they were in their 70's, and the man had a vision issue. He obviously had limited vision and was behaving very cautiously. It was time for our circus act again as we rode up to the ship and the daunting dancing stairs. We offered to let the older couple board the ship first. I had a feeling the old guy may have a problem with the stairs, and the civil servant in me wanted to be there for him if he needed help. His wife went first and got onto the ship without a problem. The man stood up holding the rail on the boat and stepped off. He missed the steps. Oh God. Out of my way. His wife was screaming and the two crew member assistants finally woke up to see what was happening. I knew they would be worthless in this situation, so I jumped up and grabbed the man around the waist to keep him from falling into the water. I got him safely on board the ship and he was thanking me profusely. Funny thing is, we never saw those two on board again. They seemed to be ghosts on the Phantom. Nothing would surprise me at this point.

Chapter Twelve

We decided to go to our cabin and get cleaned up for dinner. Oh what delightful treat were we in store for tonight? I got ready first while Rose took a snooze on the bunk. I decided to wear the red and purple skirt I brought along with my red sandals. As I finished my make-up and looked in the mirror, I thought I looked pretty darned good. As good as it gets anyway. I woke Rose and told her I would go up on deck so she would have some room to get ready.

I'm sitting on the wooden bench, looking gorgeous, and I see the Captain. He is standing at the rail looking out to sea. Don't you know, here comes the kitchen witch. They are having a conversation, but I cannot hear what they are discussing. They are not aware of my presence. I see her hand over a fistful of cash. Evidently he was getting his share of the food sale on shore to the locals. My blood starts to boil. They look over and see me staring them down, and quickly leave. I knew they were up to no good but I could not prove anything at this point. I decide to keep my eye on them and continue to observe any on-shore activity.

By this time, Rose has joined me on deck and we are both ready for dinner. We sat for a minute as I told Rose about my discovery. As we decide to get up, I look down at my feet. They are swollen twice their size and are popping out of my sandals. All that walking in the heat on shore today did not do me any good. Not only are they swollen the size of two loaves of bread, they are red as red can be. It was at that moment I figured out that my Wal-Mart sandals were not colorfast and the dye had permeated the skin on my feet. Oh great, just great! Now I was walking around with swollen, blood red feet. I was scaring fellow passengers. I had to repeat my story so many times to explain that the red dye in the sandals came off on my bread, I mean feet. What else can go wrong?

I had to ask. After dinner we decide to take in the night sky and enjoy a quiet moment on the deck. As we are sitting there on the bench of the deck, the ropes on a huge wooden boom broke and the boom swung out aimed directly at our heads. We both managed to duck in time and did not get injured. But that was only by the grace of God. We could have both been knocked out and overboard at the same time. I can't take much more excitement.

But like it or not, here came Mr. Excitement. The crew member who had the hots for Rose spots us and is walking toward us. She immediately panics and wants to get up and leave. I managed to keep her from being so obvious about her disdain for him. He plants himself next to Rose and introduces himself as Rico. He spoke with a Latin accent, and up close, he really was very good looking. Turns out he is the chief security officer on board. I could tell Rose was starting to relax with him and was enjoying the conversation. I was starting to feel like the third wheel, but I was hesitant to leave them alone. Upholding my duty as big sister, I stayed put. After an hour or so of small talk, Rico explains that he has to go on duty and must leave. However, not without further advances toward Rose. I overhear her telling him our cabin number, and I'm livid. "Rose, are you out of your mind?" "Why did you tell him our cabin number?" "Because I told him our lock was broken and he is going to see about getting it fixed for us." "You what?" "Wonderful, now I have that to worry about that too." "What do you mean? He's very sweet and I think I like him." "Never mind. Just never mind."

We decide to turn in for the night and head back to our cabin. 666. We managed to get into our bunks without too much trouble. I guess we were starting to adapt to those confined quarters. I'm lying there listening and feeling the waves crashing into the ship. It was going to be a rough night. I was imagining a storm kicking up, but without a portal, could not confirm my suspicions. In any case, I am trying very hard to get to sleep. I hear Rose snoring and knew that she wasn't going to be bothered by anything. I feel myself succumbing to exhaustion and finally drift off to sleep.

Sometime in the middle of the night I wake up to screaming. Blood -curdling screaming. What the hell? I realize it's Rose. I immediately sit straight up in bed and practically knock myself out from hitting my head on her bunk above me. In that split second, I conjure up a scenario where Rico had snuck into the cabin and is molesting Rose this very minute. He's going to have me to deal with. I jump out of the bunk, only to discover that Rose is sound asleep. She was screaming in her sleep. Unbelievable. I was very glad to see that was the case, but a part of me wanted to wake her up and shake her. But no. I leave her be and climb back into my bunk below. Another night in Paradise. What will tomorrow hold?

Chapter Thirteen

It's been four days. Her eyes are trying very hard to open and she's not sure who she sees at the end of her bed. Of course, it's Tony. He hasn't left her side the entire four days. She now sees that he's sleeping and is not aware of her awakening. Her head is hurting. Bad. She realizes her neck is in some sort of brace and she can't move her head from side to side. She can't feel her legs either. What the hell happened? What's wrong with me?

Tracey was waking up to a new reality. Her prognosis was not good and there was a chance she may never walk again. Her spine was badly injured from the accident. As she realizes she is in a hospital bed, she has the wherewithal to push the call button. A nurse appears immediately. "What time is it?" "What day is it?" "Where am I?"

"Ms. Davis, you are in Northwest General Hospital. You were in a serious accident four days ago, and you have been unconscious ever since." "Can you tell me who the President of

the United States is?" "I don't really give a crap at the moment."
"Can you tell me why I can't feel my legs?"

"Ms. Davis, you have suffered a serious spinal cord injury.
It is impacting your ability to feel or use your legs. We are not
sure yet, whether or not this will be a permanent condition."

By now, Tony is awake and standing at her side. She
looks at him in complete horror. "What the hell Tony?"
"What happened?"

"That night of the birthday party for Maggie. Remember
the storm? You were driving back to your house after the dinner
at Chi Chi's. It was pouring rain and the temperature had
dropped just enough to freeze the rain on the road. Your car
hit a tree at 60 mph. You and Jill were hurt bad.

"Jesus Christ Tony." "I don't remember any of this."
"Where is Jill?" "Is she ok?" "She's banged up pretty bad. She
has two broken arms and lots of cuts and bruises. She's home
right now." "You're the one we are all worried about." "Thank
God you've finally woken up." "I was starting to worry that you
never would."

"The cruise." "Did I miss the cruise?" "Yes, I'm afraid so,
sweetie." "That ship left three days ago." "Did everyone else
go?" "Well, of course, Jill could not make it." "I heard that Joan
decided she just couldn't go because of what happened." "What
about Maggie?" "Did Maggie go on the cruise?" "Yes. She did
Tracey. That's what I heard."

"I can't believe this. Why did this have to happen? What
am I going to do now?" "You are going to settle down and rest
yourself. You have a long recovery ahead of you, and hysterics
are not going to help. "

"Oh really?" "Screw you Tony, you're not the one lying in this bed dead from the waist down." "Tracey please. You have to calm down." This isn't helping anything."

Tracey only heard half the story. Tony realizes she didn't know the worst of it. That beautiful, perfect face would never be the same. The windshield took care of that. The panic over her legs overcame the fact that her face was entirely bandaged. I'm not sure she even realized it. My beautiful Tracey. Hollywood. How are you ever going to get through this? Well, I am going to do everything and anything I can to help you my precious. I won't leave your side. We'll get through it together.

Tracey ended up so anxious and upset that she was causing quite a scene. Her nurse came in and shot her up with some sort of sedative. She was back to sleep in a matter of seconds.

Tony uses this opportunity to leave the hospital for a quick stop in at the Center. He hasn't been at work for days, and he is starting to worry about his status with the boss. It's still raining, and the temperature is right at freezing. Tony is extra careful behind the wheel and takes his time to get there.

Upon arrival, Tony is greeted by the shift sergeant, his boss, a guy they all call Duff. Duff had heard through the grapevine about the accident and immediately inquired about Tracey and Jill. Tony started to tell Duff about the situation with Tracey, but his emotions took over as he broke down in tears. He was shaking like a leaf and could not catch his breath. Duff brought him into his office and poured him a cup of strong, black coffee. "Tony take it easy." "You don't know Duff, you don't know." "Tracey is paralyzed from the waist down and her face is really messed up. I'm not sure how bad it is because she's wrapped up like a mummy." I just left her side at the hospital. They are keeping her pretty well sedated because when she wakes up she goes nuts." "Duff she doesn't even know how bad it is." "How am I going to tell her?" "Tony, you don't have to be the one to tell her." "Let the professionals handle that at the hospital." "All you have to do is be there for her." "That's what she is going to need to get through this." "You by her side." "You can go on leave so you can be with her." "I appreciate that Duff, but I'm not sure I can take it 24/7. Work will be a good distraction for me." "I think I'll keep on the schedule if you don't mind." "Sure." "I really do need you here, you know that." I just want to help however I can." "Well if you could be flexible with my coming and going, I'll do my best to put in a full shift." "How are things anyway?" "Oh you really don't want to know Tony." "It's crazier than ever up there." "Funding has been cut so we've had to cut back on staff. We are trying to keep the peace as best we can, but the inmates see opportunity to stir up hostility. They know we are short-staffed and they are going to take advantage of that fact any way they can think of.

"And it's not only the inmates that are causing us trouble." "You know that guy they brought in a couple months ago? The "Family" guy with all the outside connections?" "Yeah I remember." "Isn't his name Pauly?" "Yeah that's right, Pauly." "What's up with him?" "Well, the other day this guy comes up to the visitation desk." "He's wearing a wig, sunglasses and a long fur coat. Swear to God Tony." "You would not have believed this." He's gone right past the Control Room without any interference, and is proceeding to walk right past the visitation desk without checking in or anything." "So I stop him and ask what he thinks he's doing." "He tells me he is Pauly's son." "So that being the case, I figured I better let him pass." "You know we've been ordered not to interfere with the Spaghetti Gang." "So he goes in to see Pauly and he starts pulling stuff out of his coat." "And by stuff, I mean salamis, pepperoni, cheese, bread, olives." "This guy was a walking delicatessen" "I had to look the other way, but not before I saw everything he managed to bring into that pod for Pauly." "I tell you, this guy Pauly must have dirty pictures of somebody." "He seems to get whatever he wants in here and no one has any say over what's going on." "It's really making me crazy."

"And that's not the worst of it. With all his connections, Pauly gets the OK from the Warden to have a conjugal visit with his wife. You know that's unheard of but somehow he pulls this off." "So a few days ago, she shows up." "This broad looks like she just stepped out of Saks Fifth Avenue. " "She is dressed to the nines, dripping in diamonds, in a pair of heels that had to be 8" high." "She had a set of jugs like you never saw, and her ass was as tight as a sailors bunk in boot camp." "I'm telling you, she caused a raucous walking through the pod on her way to see Pauly. We practically had to hose them down."

"So Frankie is on duty up there and he puts the two of them into a solitary cell with a solid door with no windows." "He tells them they have 30 minutes." "Pauly is practically drooling at this point." "Frankie sits outside the door making sure they are not disturbed." "No more than ten minutes into the visit, Frankie hears a blood curdling scream." "Pauly is screaming and swearing at the top of his lungs." "You bitch!" "Get out!" "Get out of here now." "Frankie jumps up, opens the door, and sees

Pauly bent over holding his face, blood everywhere, and the wife spitting up in the corner of the room." "Here, she bit his nose off Tony." "That bitch came in and bit his nose off." There it was, lying in the corner of the room and Pauly was hysterical." "Frankie runs over to Pauly and calls for back-up and medical assistance." "The wife proceeds to calmly leave the pod and heads for the exit." "Luckily Joan had her wits about her and stopped the bitch before she reached the door."

"Holy shit, Duff!" "That's some crazy shit!" "Where is the bitch now?" "She's locked up with the rest of them." "I hear she's not too fond of her orange ensemble." "Yeah, I bet." "No spike heels or diamonds in this place." "You can't tell her from any of the other broads in here." "Yeah, they're all the same to me…royal pains in my ass." "I'll be doing my best to make sure I come nowhere near that bitch."

Chapter Fourteen

Day Five at Sea

Day five on The Phantom, and we are actually falling into a routine. We understand and obey the rules. Eat what you get, don't ask for seconds, and don't question anything. Above all, don't wear shoes on the ship. Boy, we learned that one the hard way. I wouldn't say we were having fun, but at least we now knew the score around there. Or, we thought we did.

My observant, pessimistic, suspicious character traits cannot be on vacation as hard as I try. It seems, where I go, trouble follows. The Phantom was no exception.

The Captain of this rusted out wreck of a ship was very seldom seen. It was as if he was deliberately trying to stay out of sight. The only interaction passengers had with him was listening to his daily diatribe on the loud speaker. Announcing port of call and scheduled departure times. I did know who he was, only because I saw him that one time with the kitchen witch, and I recognized his particular uniform as representative of

Captains rank. He wasn't able to stay out of my view. I was watching him and did not like what I was seeing. Every stop we made involved a visitor to see the Captain. He was having private meetings in a locked room in every port we stopped at. I know this, because I've been observing it. The first stop and foreign visitor was my initial internal red flag. I could see something didn't look right. And beyond that, I could feel it in my gut. That familiar "oh shit" feeling that I got so often at the Justice Center. Something bad is happening here and I am compelled to see what I can do to stop it.

I tried to access the Captain's quarters that served as their private meeting room late one afternoon, but found it locked and inaccessible. I could not get in there to check it out, but that would not stop me from continuing to pursue this situation. Something criminal was going on onboard this ship and I was determined to uncover it. I had the feeling that the kitchen witch was in on it, and she was my second observation interest.

The evening was upon us and Rose and I decided to see what the onboard entertainment was. Of course we there was no professional entertainment. Our options were to get sloshed on rum punch or take part in the passenger participation game play. Since rum was just one of the alcohols I was allergic to, we opted for the game play.

We went upstairs to the main deck and took a seat on the bench. Most everyone was there including the Captain. Oddly enough, he was front and center in the activities and seemed to be singling me out for some reason. Music was blaring and everyone else had had their share of the rum punch. It seems we arrived just in time for a game that I knew I wanted no part of.

However, the Captain, as the leader of the activity, was pointing to me and asking that I join him in the circle to kick off the game. Of course, I refused, but he was having none of that. He kept insisting that I join him. I really had no choice so I gave in and joined him in the center of the circle of passengers that had formed for the game.

It didn't take long to understand the objective of the game. There were two teams. A very long rope was passed around the circle from passenger to passenger. When you received the rope, you were to put it through your clothes and then pass it on to the next person in the circle. The team that got the rope through the last person first would be the winner. As the rope went around the circle, it got shorter and shorter and tighter and tighter around everyone's clothes. This was causing your clothes to constrict. It was too late to do anything when I realized what was happening. I was a sitting, or should I say standing, duck. My shirt was going up and up and my pants were going down and down. My size H girls were exposed for the world to see and my granny panties were causing hysterical fits of laughter around the circle. This was happening to everyone in the circle, even though I felt as if I was the brunt of the Captain's sick sense of humor. He knew very well what would happen and he set me up. Needless to say I was totally mortified even though my precious sister was falling on the deck laughing at me, really enjoying my pain. Even though she was suffering the same fate that the rope was having on me, her cute, sexy, matching underwear was more of a treat to our fellow passengers than my XXL, functional, do-the-job underwear that was causing such hysterical laughter for all who witnessed my attack. There were so many people in the circle that the game went on forever. I could not wait to get out of there and back to our cabin. This whole scene made me more determined than ever to get back at the Captain. He will pay for this. Believe me, he will pay.

Chapter Fifteen

I wake up to the sound of the breakfast bell ringing. My single crab cake dinner was not enough to fill me up last night and I went to bed hungry. So by now, I'm starving. My hunger is offset, however, by the anger I still feel as the brunt of last night's cruel audience participation prank. How can I face my fellow passengers today? I swear if I hear one little snicker, I am going to go off. Rose is still enjoying the memory of my mortification. Hers is the snicker I have to endure. I know she will never let me live it down. It will be the topic of many family gatherings to come. Why is it always me? Why do I always **find myself in the center of a "situation?"**

Last night's antics, took me back to the time when I let my generous spirit take me to a place that I had no business going. The crew at the jail was a tight bunch. We always had each other's back and would pretty much do anything to help a fellow officer. When we got the word that Sgt. Wells had stage four cancer of the prostate, we could not ignore the need to help him out. Wells was out on unpaid sick leave for six months, and we all knew he was struggling with the hospital bills. He had four little kids ranging in age from two years to ten years old. He and his wife were fighting hard to keep it all together, but it didn't take long for his mortgage to go into arrears. He was on the verge of losing his house. We just could not let that happen.

So the word went out. We needed to find a way to help Wells and his family save their house. We had to raise some big money fast. None of us earned much of a salary. We would all be in the same boat if that happened to us. But there was one exception. O'Neal. In addition to serving as Staff Sgt. for the County Corrections Center, O'Neal owned a bar down on Payne Avenue. It wasn't in the best of neighborhoods, but he seemed to be making a go of it. You might say that was because of the "entertainment" the bar offered to his patrons. You see, O'Neal ran a mud wrestling ring in the basement of his bar. Every weekend he featured an event of interest. What made it interesting were the side bets going on that were lining the pockets of participating spectators. I knew there had to be a way to use O'Neal's mud wrestling arena to raise money for Wells. So I went down to Payne Avenue after work one night with Duff. We met with O'Neal and asked him about using this event night as a way to raise money for Wells. He was on board immediately and definitely bought some creative marketing ideas to the table. O'Neal saw the opportunity to get the C.O.'s involved. His idea was to promote mud wrestling matches that featured one man against two women in tournament -type elimination rounds to the top slot. In an effort to make the match fair, the men had to fight on their knees with boxing gloves on. Whether or not that made it fair was debatable, but it sure made it interesting. O'Neal would need CO volunteers to match up for the tournament. Both men and women. O'Neal thought Duff and I could be the featured contenders. He was sure that would bring out every CO in the department to witness that circus act. He would charge $20.00 a ticket and all the money raised would go to Wells and his family. He also promised to give the house share of all bets to the cause as well as any profits he made on drink sales. This could mean big money. It all sounded like a sure fire way to raise some big bucks for the Wells family. But there was one fly in the ointment here. There was no way I was going to volunteer to get in that mud pit. Believe me; I was all for helping raise the money here, but that was just one step too far that I was not going to take for anybody. Duff, on the other hand, was all for the idea. He was willing to sacrifice his dignity as shift supervisor to take on two women in a mud match. What a surprise.

Our next step was recruiting CO's for the event. We knew we would get our share of guys, but getting women participants was going to be the challenge. Once the word went out about our pending fund raising event, the volunteers started to come forward. To our amazement, we did get two women volunteers. CO's Karen and Ellen. That was a relief. Better them than me. The event was scheduled for the Saturday night before Thanksgiving. Mud Mania was upon us.

O'Neal's intuition was right on. Virtually every officer who was not on duty that night, showed up at his place to witness Mud Mania. I was looking forward to it myself. I couldn't wait to see Duff in the buff trying to prove his manhood against two female officers in the featured match. This was going to be epic. The bleachers were full of drunked up spectators. The chanting started low but got louder and louder. It was like a coliseum full of Romans calling for the lions to meet the gladiators. The first couple matches were guy vs. guy. It was fun to watch, but everyone was waiting for the ladies to hit the mud. Duff was backstage pumping himself up for the big event. His adversaries were MIA. Where were Karen and Ellen? Our volunteer lady officers. It seemed they decided not to show at the last minute and the whole event was in jeopardy. The next thing I know, here comes O'Neal right up to me. Somehow I knew what he was going to say. "Maggie, we need you to get in the pit with Duff. Karen and Ellen are no-shows, and this place will go crazy if we don't have a ladies match. You've got to do it. Please Maggie. Do it for Wells." How could I refuse? After all, it was for Wells. I thought about those four little Wells kids out on the street, and that was all it took. I really couldn't believe I was doing it, but there I was backstage, taking off my clothes and putting on a toga to go into the mud pit. It was one on one. Me against Duff. Just as O'Neal had hoped. When I came out into that mud pit, the place went ape shit. It was mass pandemonium.

Duff never had a chance. I let him play at trying to bring me down. All he did was kick up the mud so that I was covered from head to toe. I had mud in places I can't even say. My face, my hair, my hoo hoo. You name it. It was covered in dark brown, slippery, disgusting mud. I had just about enough of it. Time to bring Duff face down in the mud. I had him on the ground with one twist of his arm. I sat on his gut while the ref counted to 10. It was no contest. The Mud Hen won this one. That was my new nickname for months. Mud Hen. I didn't mind. We raised $4,500 for Wells and saved his house from the auction block. This was another one of those "situations" that will never be forgotten. As bad as it was for me, it was worse for Duff. He lost to the Mud Hen. Too bad for Duff.

Chapter Sixteen

We did manage to get showered and dressed and ascend the ladder to the dining deck. It is a beautiful morning. I have to say that has been the best part of this cruise...the weather. Never have I seen such blue skies. Not a cloud in sight. And the water is multi shades of blue and teal. Absolutely stunning.

As we maneuver ourselves to the end of the "buffet" line, I see the Captain and the kitchen witch conferring in a corner. It appears they are conspiring to have another mystery guest meeting. We are just arriving in the Port of St. John's Island and I expect they will be conducting further business with a local visitor.

I feel the bump of the ship meeting the dock so I know we have landed. I haven't even had my second bite of my breakfast delight when I see him coming up the entry way. Talk about creepy. This guy looks like he could turn you to stone with one look in his eye. I did my best not to make eye contact with this character. I did not want him to remember me looking at him.

He makes a beeline for the Captains quarters and I see the kitchen witch following close behind. He is carrying a large, leather, beat up satchel. They both enter the Captains quarters and I hear the door lock. This is a private, confidential meeting for sure. It appears St. John's will be a lucrative stop for our Captain.

Rose and I manage to hang around the dining deck unnoticed. This gives me the chance to observe. We linger over breakfast for about an hour and that's all it takes for the secret meeting to disband. I see the Captain's door open and the creepy local guy is leaving sans the satchel.

Suspecting what I know must be happening, I start to think about a way that I can break into the Captain's quarters in order to see what's in that satchel. This will take some careful planning and I don't have much time. St. Martin's is our final stop on this cruise. We will be heading back to Antigua in two days for final disembarkment. Somehow I have got to get the goods on this guy.

As I ponder a course of action, Rose is confronted once again with Rico. Here he comes sauntering up the deck. He sits down beside her and turns on the charm. I can't believe she is being taken in by this guy, but there she is all flustered and flirty. Give me a break already. Don't I have enough to worry about here? How is she going to help me bust the Captain if she is all taken up with this suave sailor? And then it comes to me. Rico. As chief security officer, he has keys to every cabin. Including the Captain's. We have to bring him in on this. He can help us. I'm sure of it.

Chapter Seventeen

What a gorgeous morning. Rose and I are taking in the beauty of the sunrise against the dark waters of the ocean and the starlit sky. This breathtaking sight overwhelms me with a spiritual connection to the universe and appreciation for this God given gift of peaceful beauty. I cannot help but think about Tracey and Jill and wonder how they are. I pray for their recovery and ask God to help them deal with the aftermath of this awful tragedy. I start to cry uncontrollably and Rose is not sure what is going on. "Maggie, what's wrong?" "Why are you crying?" "I'm thinking about my friends at home in the hospital." "I am so worried about them." "I'm not sure they will understand why I went on this trip without them and I hope they will forgive me." "Listen, it's not like they are missing some fabulous trip here. This cruise has been a nightmare. They will probably be glad they didn't go once you tell them all about our experience here." "You have to admit we are lucky to be alive. And I don't know about you, but I can't wait to get off this rusted bucket of bolts and get home."

"I know." "You're right." "They have no idea what we are going through right now." "I just feel so guilty knowing what they are going through."

Rose and I did our best to work in some sort of exercise every day. I figured with the severe rationing of food this week, with a little effort to exercise, maybe I could lose a few pounds. We decided to walk around the deck after breakfast. We stop at the back of the ship and watch the sea gulls following closely. They dip and dive in the wake trying desperately to get near the ship. At first it was fun to watch them trying desperately to get closer. But then I realized the kitchen crew was throwing scraps and garbage off this ship right into the ocean. Further evidence of this no-class operation. Not only were they risking the safety of the passengers and crew, they were violating maritime law that prohibits dumping into ocean waters. Note to self, this needs to be documented, recorded, and possibly used as leverage against the Captain and the Kitchen Witch. Not only is it illegal, it's downright nasty.

We completed 10 laps around the deck and I was just about spent. Rose could have done another 10 and I told her to have at it. She decided to quit when I did. After all it was God awful hot. Had to be 100 degrees in the shade that day. I was desperate for a drink. I knew there was no chance of getting anything other than a Dixie cup full of warm water. It will have to do. I tried to make it last. The Kitchen Witch was on duty and I was not in the mood to confront her.

Chapter Eighteen

On his way to the hospital Tony drove through McDonalds for a couple of coffees and two sausage, egg, McMuffins. One for him and one for Tracey. Today was the day her facial bandages were coming off. She was aware of this impending situation, and was now fully able to understand the seriousness of what could be the underlying issue. Her face. Her beautiful face. Was it totally destroyed? God forbid. Tony had to be there for her. It did not matter to him what she looked like. His love for her went way beyond the physical beauty. Over the last four days, Tony did a lot of soul searching. He came to realize how much Tracey meant to him and he was committed to getting back into her life permanently. He wanted to help her get through this traumatic time as the husband he never was before. He wanted the chance to prove to her that he would be her rock. He would take care of her and love her unconditionally forever. If only she would let him.

She was awake and waiting for him when he got to her room. He took it as a good sign that she was hungry and devoured the muffin. As they drank their coffee together, Dr. Tyler entered the room. He was accompanied by two nurses and an assistant medical student.

"Good morning Tracey." "Is it?" "Yes it is. Today we take off your facial bandages and begin the journey of healing. "Don't talk to me about journeys." "That's what started this whole mess." "Okay, poor choice of words there. Sorry about that." "Nevertheless, today is a day to be noted in your calendar. Because six weeks from today, I expect you will look totally different than you do today." "Better or worse?" "Oh, it will be remarkable Tracey." "The bruising and swelling will be just about gone and we will be in a position to understand what comes next." "What does that mean?" "Well, I expect you will be having some plastic surgery at some point to diminish any scaring that remains from the accident." "How bad will the scaring be Doc?" "Well, let's have a look, shall we."

The nurses brought a tray of instruments over to Dr. Tyler. He puts a light band around his head so he can see her face totally lit up and magnetized. Tracey closes her eyes tightly as Tony grabs both her hands. He holds her and whispers gently to her that everything's going to be okay. "No matter how you look Tracey, you will always be the most beautiful woman in the world to me." "I will never leave your side." As Dr. Tyler begins to unravel the bandages around her head, Tracey winces in pain. At one point she screams out and begs him to stop. She can't take it. The pain is immense, but the fear is even worse. She is so afraid of what she will see when she looks in the mirror.

Ever so slowly, the bandages are unwrapped. Around and around her head, closer and closer to revealing her new reality.

At last they are finally off. Tony tries with all his might to keep smiling. He is dying inside. Dr. Tyler wants to speak to Tracey before she is allowed to have a mirror. He gently tells her that right now her face is unrecognizable. He assures her that this is only temporary. As she continues to heal, the swelling, bruising, and contusions will diminish. Slowly. He assures her that he can help her get back the face she knows. The beautiful face that turned heads in any room she entered. Tony's fear was she would still be turning heads, but not because she was so beautiful. He was heartbroken and could not find the words to comfort Tracey. He continued to hold both her hands when Dr. Tyler gave her the mirror. She took one look and began screaming. "No! No! That isn't me!"

"Yes it is you Tracey." "The same beautiful you you've always been." "What you see in that mirror is the same person that I love. The same person that has so many friends who love her. That is not going to change. You have people who love you that will stand by you as you recover from this. And you will recover Tracey. You have to believe that. Listen to Dr. Tyler. It's just a matter of time. In a few months you will look like you always have. Hollywood. No doubt."

"I'm a monster." "No one is going to want to look at me. I can't even look at myself. I can't be seen by anyone. Please Tony, don't let anyone in here. I mean it. No one. Promise me." Tracey is sobbing uncontrollably. She is going into hysterics and Dr. Tyler cannot allow that. He injects a sedative into her IV and she immediately goes back to sleep.

"Dr. Tyler, what can I do to help her?" "How can I help her cope with this and do what she needs to recover?" "The best thing you can do Tony is to be here for her. She has to know that people love her and want to be with her." "This is going to be extremely rough for Tracey." "A beautiful woman like her will not accept the image she sees in the mirror now. She will need to be monitored 24/7 to be sure she doesn't try to hurt herself further. "She will feel desperate, isolated, and abandoned." "Her friends and family need to rally behind her and help her through this challenging time." "Injuries like hers can take years to heal completely." "She will need to be patient and understand this." "We will do what we can to help her, but she will need far reaching support from all who know and love her."

"Well, consider me number one on that list Doc. I'll be here for her and do whatever I can. How long will she stay asleep now?" "She'll be out for a few hours Tony." "If you want to go home and freshen up, now would be a good time." "I'll do that Doc, but I'll be back before she wakes up again." "Okay Tony, but you cannot take this on alone here. You need to reach out to her friends and family and get a support plan in place. Everyone needs to do their part." "You're right Doc, and I know just where to begin."

Chapter Nineteen

Rose and I are up early. After taking turns to get showered and ready for the day, we make our way to the dining room for breakfast. We are in for a real treat this morning. Along with our usual mystery meat breakfast sandwich, we are given a slice of mango and two chunks of pineapple. Amazing. I never knew fruit could taste so good. I'm feeling good about today. I'm going to figure out what's really going on around here and bring some law and order to this ship. As we are enjoying the last of our coffee, we are joined by Rico. It seems he and Rose enjoyed some time alone last night after I went to bed. Dancing on deck in the moonlight with a secret glass of wine has created a bond between them that I'm not sure I like. Rose, however, is totally taken by Rico. It's very obvious she's fallen for him and it appears the feeling is mutual. I decide to make this work to our advantage. Let's see how far Rico will go to impress his new love.

"Good morning Rico." "How are you this fine morning?" "I am good Maggie, how are you?" "Oh you know...pretty good seeing that this is our last full day on this tug." "So tell me Rico, have you ever noticed the shenanigans that go on here with the Captain, the kitchen witch, and all these mystery visitors that come on board in every port?" "Shenanigans?" "I do not know what that means." "Oh sorry, that's my Irish showing." "Shenanigans means activity of the delinquent kind." "Sorry, still don't know what you mean." "You know, shady, underhanded, sneaky." "Things going on that aren't right." "Things that may be illegal and cause for criminal charges." "Hey, I am not involved in any of that." "You know that right Maggie?" "Yes, Rico, I know you are not involved and are innocent of any wrong doing." "But your Captain, and his kitchen witch, now that's another story." "They have some kind of a scheme going on that my gut is telling me is illegal." "You know I have a sixth sense about these things."

"Yes, Rose has told me that." "If that's what you think, why are you telling me all this?" "Because we need your help Rico. I intend to bust up this little operation, and I will need your help to do so." "My help." "What do you think I can do to help you?" "Well, as head Security Officer, I'm guessing you have a key to every door on this ship. Is that right?" "Yes, as a matter of fact, I do." "Including the Captains quarters?" "Yes, I have a key to his quarters as well." "Great! That's what I was hoping to hear."

"Our next port stop is St. Martin's." "If all goes as usual, there will be a visitor to the ship coming on board right after breakfast is all cleaned up. Whoever it is will be met on the deck by the kitchen witch and escorted right into the Captain's quarters. They will most likely be carrying a satchel of some sort. That's what I have observed in the last few port stops we've made. They will meet together in his cabin for about forty-five minutes. Then the visitor will go back on shore, but without the satchel he came with. That satchel will be in the Captain's quarters, and I intend to get a look inside to see what he's up to." "Oh I get it." "You think I can get you inside the Captain's cabin with my master key huh?" "That's right Rico. Now you're getting the idea here. We have to get him with the goods if we want to make the charges stick." "Charges, what charges are you talking about?" "I intend to have the Captain and his kitchen witch arrested for violation of maritime law in the illegal transport and sale of opioids. That's what I suspect is going on here. You could fit an awful lot of tiny, little, illegal pills in a satchel of that size. Probably a couple million dollars' worth anyway. He is bringing them on board in every port. By the time we complete the island circuit and sail back to Antigua, he's going to have quite a large supply. "Let's say he has picked up two million dollars' worth of pills in every port we've landed in. That means he's hiding ten million dollars' worth of illegal narcotics in his cabin. I know for a fact that there is a large circuit of drug runners that work between Antigua and Miami. All he has to do is make it to Antigua with the goods, and the mob will take it from there. He is their mule. He makes the supply available to them with all his island contacts who meet him at every port. What an operation he's got going on here." "What appears to be a broken down barefoot cruise line on its last leg so to speak, is really a cog in the wheel of a huge illegal narcotics operation." "We are just the pawns who are unwillingly a part of his phantom cruise line." "We actually paid money to be part of it." "What a rip off."

"Okay, okay, Maggie." "Just hang on here a minute. Aren't you jumping to conclusions here?" "How do you know that's what's inside the satchel bags?" "What makes you so sure you have this all figured out?"

"Well Rico, that's where you come in." "You have to inspect the Captain's quarters and see if you can find the stash." "I'm sure it will not be in plain sight. He will have hidden it somehow in his cabin. We need you to find the goods. Take pictures of it all when you find it and then make arrangements for the police to meet us in Antigua. They can arrest them both and we can lead them to the stash. We are going to shut this operation down once and for all."

"That would be the end of my job here Maggie." "What am I supposed to do for work if the Captain gets locked up and is not running this cruise line anymore?" "Let's not worry about that right now Rico." "Easy for you to say Maggie." "This job is my livelihood. It's all I have. You know there is not a lot of security work in Antigua." "I really liked my position on this ship." "My job was to walk among all the beautiful passengers and assure them that their security was guaranteed and that they could feel safe on board." "It really was a piece of cake you know." "Yeah, I guess so Rico. You obviously did not monitor the Captain at all. That's where all the action was and you didn't even know it. It took two Irish sisters to come on board to uncover what was going on right under your nose." "Listen Maggie. I'll do whatever you need me to do. Just don't implicate me in this mess. As you said, I knew nothing about it. "Embarrassing but true."

"I'm relatively sure I can enter and search the Captain's quarters if you and Rose can distract him and keep the kitchen witch busy as well. When do you want to pull this off?" "It has to be today. We know that right after breakfast the visitor will board the ship with the satchel. You take pictures of the guy getting on board and entering the Captain's quarters." Later today, when most of the passengers leave for their shore excursions, Rose and I will stay behind. We'll cook up some situation that will demand the attention of the Captain and the kitchen witch outside of his quarters and the galley. Somewhere on the front deck. That will be your opportunity to go into his cabin and find the stash. Once you know where it's hiding and have taken pictures of it all, come out to where we are and join us. Then you can handcuff them both. You can deliver them to officials in Antigua and you'll have all the evidence you need for an open and shut case.

Chapter Twenty

The door to her hospital room was closed. Just like the curtains on the windows. Tracey was doing her best to shut out the world. She could not bear to look at herself and she didn't want anyone else looking at her either. She was barely eating enough to keep herself alive and her activity was limited to trips to the nearby bathroom. The nurses taped a towel over the bathroom mirror so she could not see her reflection as she entered. They really were going to all lengths to make sure Tracey could get through this. She didn't watch television. She didn't read. She mostly just sat in her dimly lit room. Thinking. Thinking. Thinking. She was driving herself mad. She blamed no one but herself for what happened. If only she didn't have that last margarita. If only it wasn't raining that night. If only she wasn't speeding to get home quicker. Why? Why? Why?

Tracey heard something but could not distinguish what it was. There, again. She realizes it was a knock on her door. A very light knock that she barely heard. Whoever it is can just go away. She is not about to answer the door much less let anyone in her room to see her.

"Tracey." "You in there?" "It's me, Tony." "I have a surprise for you." Before she can even respond the door is slammed open and she is revealed to the world. There in a wheelchair sits Jill. Tony has brought her to see Tracey. Jill is grinning ear to ear and appears to be the happiest person on earth. She extends both arms as Tony wheels her closer to Tracey. Best friends. Together again. Hugging each other and sobbing.

"Tracey I am so happy to see you." "Oh really? Do you like what you see?" "No, I love what I see." "I see my best friend alive and kicking. I still have you. I was so afraid I was going to lose you Tracey. You mean the world to me and I could not go on living if I didn't have you." "Jill, I can't even stand to look in the mirror. How am I going to go on living? How can you even want to be my best friend? Aren't you appalled by what you see here? I'm a monster. I don't want you here. Don't bother me. Please go. Get out of here and leave me alone."

"Oh no you don't." "You don't get to dismiss me like that. I'm not going anywhere. We are going to get through this together just like we always have. We are both going to recover. We are going to come out of this mess stronger, braver, and more committed to each other than ever. It's going to take strength and bravery to come back from this Tracey. We are stronger and braver when we are together. We always have been and this is no exception. So get ready to be bothered. I'm going to bother you every day. I'm going to bother the heck out of you until the day that we are walking out of this place together. So start eating. You need to build up your strength. Open up those blinds and turn up the lights. Look in that mirror and smile. Because you are alive Tracey. And so is your best friend. We're still together and as beautiful as ever.

Tony took a big chance here. He wasn't sure how this reunion was going to go, but he could not have hoped for a better outcome. Jill is just the medicine that Tracey needs.

Chapter Twenty-One

Breakfast service is just about done and we are about to dock in the port of St. Martin Island. Passengers are antsy to get off the tug for their excursions. Rose and I are laying low on deck outside the dining room. We have a clear view of the Captain's quarters, but we are not too obviously visible. Rico is standing by on the deck with his Polaroid camera at the ready. Deck hands are wrangling the tug against the dock. They finally get the ropes over the stanchions as we nestle against the dock. We've landed. As passengers are pouring off the ship we see our expected visitor boarding against the flow of the crowd. Satchel strapped to his side. He heads right for the Captain's quarters escorted by the kitchen witch. Rose and I are watching this scenario coming down, and Rico is casually taking photos of him, his satchel, and his entrance into the Captain's quarters. The meeting is in progress and we start timing it. Sure enough, forty-five minutes later our guest visitor is getting ready to depart. Rico's camera is capturing the farewell handshakes with a nice clear picture of the three of them. Partners in crime. So we know the goods are on board once again. This makes five port stops, and I am estimating a stash of around ten million dollars. I can't wait to expose this thug and his sidekick.

We allow some time to pass so that everyone assumes its business as usual. Nothing to be alarmed about. Rose and I are about to cause some alarm that's going to bring anyone left on board running toward the ruckus to see what's going on.

She wasn't too crazy about the idea, but I talked Rose into feigning a fall overboard, right into a lifeboat that is precariously hanging on rope about twenty feet down from the deck. The plan was for her to shimmy down the rope; plop herself in the boat and start screaming out in agony that she is sure she broke her ankle. The sure fire attraction was the fact that Rose was going to lose her bikini top on the way down. No doubt this is a distraction that no man on board could resist. There is no way I could have pulled this off. I never would have made it down the rope and if by some chance I did, the lifeboat would have plunged into the water. I knew the weight of Rose would keep the lifeboat dangling off the side of the ship while I stood on deck looking over at her and screaming at the top of my lungs. Of course, she did her share of screaming too. There she was. Her boobs were naked to the world. I knew she was mortified but she left herself exposed just long enough to get all of the crew to the side of the ship.

The first one on the scene was Rico. He pulled the alarm. This demands the Captain's attention to the matter. He is next on the scene followed closely by the kitchen witch. Reluctantly, Rico leaves the scene in order to secure the help of a few other deck hands. It's quite hectic, loud, and chaotic and Rose is pulling off quite a dramatic injury scene. I never knew she was such a good actress. I am doing my part by screaming at everyone on scene to help Rose. "Pull up that lifeboat." "We have to get her out of there. She is hurt bad." We knew this antiquated old tug did not have any type of hydraulic lift system and required all hands on deck to manually pull on the ropes to raise the lifeboat up onto the deck. This was no easy task. Everyone is doing their part to help pull up the lifeboat. The Captain, the kitchen witch, all the deck hands, they were all pulling on the ropes with all their strength. There was one obvious absence that I am hoping is busy elsewhere. It was our job to keep this chaos going for as long as possible so that Rico could do his part with the camera in the Captain's quarters. Rico had no problem getting into the Captain's quarters and quickly went to work searching for the hidden stash. Rummaging through every desk drawer, checking out every closet and obvious hiding place, he was coming up with nothing. Rico was starting to panic when he noticed the rug under the Captain's desk was not centered as it usually was. He could hear the screaming on deck continuing, so he knew he had some time to investigate. He kicks back the rug exposing the floor boards, and sure enough he sees one that appears to be ever so slightly raised up. He pulls up on it and four floor boards come popping out at once. He can't believe his eyes. There it was. A leather box with a sliding lid. He pulls the lid back and exposes the content of the box. It's opioid nirvana. There had to be hundreds of thousands of little white pills. Maggie was right all along. This was definitely a sophisticated operation that was going on for years. Rico gets busy with the camera and documents everything he sees. He quickly puts everything back the way it was and rejoins the crew on deck, still trying to pull up the lifeboat with Rose in tow. Rose had to move her arms upward to reach for help, once again exposing the girls. This proved to be the icing on the cake. Not one of those guys, including the Captain, moved away from that lifeboat until I threw Rose her cover up to put on. Once the show was over, most of them went back to their stations. A subtle wink from Rico tells me that he got what he needed. Rose continues to carry on at a fearful rate as the lifeboat is finally landed on the deck. Rico jumps into action and lifts Rose out of the boat and into his arms. She is sobbing and hanging on to him for dear life. Rico takes charge of the situation as you would expect the Head Security Officer to do. He barks orders at the crewmen to get the lifeboat back where it belonged and assured the Captain that he would see to Rose and take care of her immediate needs. The Captain was only too happy to exit the scene and get back to his quarters. He arrives to find his locked door secure and once inside does not notice anything out of place. He has no clue. This is good.

Rico has all the evidence we need to lock this guy up for a long time. He carries Rose into our cabin and I barricade the door. We are alone to share the details of his adventure. Rose has stopped screaming, crying, and carrying on as she is totally unharmed from the whole scenario. Rico shows us the photos he has of the stash in the Captain's quarters. I knew it! Just as I suspected, we are all sailing along with an illegal fortune in drugs. Now we need Rico to make contact with officials in Antigua so that they are waiting with handcuffs for the Captain as soon as we land in port.

Chapter Twenty-Two

Jill and Tracey are once again joined at the hip. Their joint physical therapy sessions have turned into a friendly contest to see who can progress further and faster. The hospital staff is amazed at the progress both girls have made in such a short time. It was only a matter of time before they start to wonder about Maggie and the cruise. "I wonder if she's back yet." "Do you think she had a good time?" "I can't wait to hear all about it." "Well, either she's home by now, or she will be in a day or so." "I've kind of lost track of things with all this tragedy going on." "Yeah, me too." "Did you know though that Joan decided not to go on the trip?" "No." "I hadn't heard that from any one." "You mean she's been home all this time?" "Yeah. She actually came to see me a few days ago." "She said she was just too upset by everything to even think of going on the trip. Said there was no way she would enjoy herself." "Well, I guess it didn't stop Maggie though huh?" "You know Maggie. She's not going to let anything or anybody get in the way of her plans."

"That girl has a strong constitution." "I'll say." Oh, and Joan told me that Maggie brought her sister Rose on the cruise with her." "Well, I'm glad she had someone to go with her." "I'm sure she didn't want to go by herself." "I hope she had a good time." "At least one of us got to go." "Do you think she'll come see us when she gets back?" "Ah, yeah!" "I'm sure she will." "Well, I sure hope so." "I can't wait to hear about her trip."

"Hello there." "Two of my favorite ladies." "What's up today?" "I am so happy you brought Jill down here to be with me." "She helps me forget how awful I feel and we've been laughing together quite a bit lately." "Glad to hear that Tracey." "What is it you find so amusing?" "Well, we are just imagining the awesome trip that Maggie and her sister went on without us."

"She's got to be on her way home by now I think," "So do you think you could try and reach her Tony and let her know that Jill and I would like her to come visit us so we can hear all about the trip?" "Of course." "I'll reach out later today and see if she's home yet. I'm sure she would be happy to come visit you guys.

Chapter Twenty-Three

"What do we do now Rose?" "Don't ask me." "Maggie is the professional here." "What do you think Maggie?" "Well, Rico, you have to radio through to Antigua Port Authority and have them reach out to the local police department. You can explain the whole scenario and let them know you have pictures to document your story. I'm sure they will be anxious to collar these two when you tell them how much opioid inventory they have sitting on this wreck. They all need to meet us at the port when we arrive, but tell them to stay out of sight until you signal them to board. " "Maggie, I'm going to go pack now. I still have a lot to do to get ready to go and all this talk about authorities and criminals makes me very nervous. " "Okay Rose, you go ahead, I'll join you in a few minutes to get my own packing done."

"How does the disembarking process work Rico?" "Procedure calls for all passengers to disembark first." "The crew, including the Captain, stays on board until they have all quarters cleaned and the kitchen is cleaned and stocked for the next sail."

"Okay, that's good. Very good." "So while the crew is busy cleaning up, you can go on shore and get the authorities." "Then you can escort them right into the Captain's quarters. Just be sure a few go directly into the kitchen too so that witch doesn't escape." "So we have a plan. I'm going to go and pack all my stuff because once this comes down, I won't have a place on this ship anymore." "My job goes away and I have no idea what I'm going to do now." "Don't worry Rico." "I've got a few ideas on that front." "Just trust me will you?" "I guess I have to Maggie. What else can I do at this point?" "Well, for one thing, you can tell me how serious you are about Rose." "Do you have feelings for her Rico? Serious feelings?" "Yes I do Maggie. I can't believe it's happened myself, but I've fallen in love with Rose." "She is the most beautiful, innocent, sweetest girl I have ever met." "She makes me so happy when I am with her." "I don't know if I can let her go." "Well, maybe you won't have to Rico."

The ship's horn is bellowing the signal that we are about to dock in the port of Antigua. Thank God. I have no idea how we survived a week on this tug, but no one will be happier to get off than me. Passengers are lining up at the exit gate. Rose and I are hanging back on the lower deck. We plan to be the last two off so that Rico knows when to signal the shore patrol. We can see from our position that our fellow passengers are exiting in a nice orderly fashion. Then I spot the Captain and the kitchen witch together on the ship's bow waving everyone off. I'm sure they are anxious to get their cache together and organized for the big payoff.

The last two passengers in the line are the elderly couple that we helped out in the excursion boat. I guess they stayed on through the end even though we hadn't seen them since St. John. Two crew members were helping them down the gang-plank toward the dock when two big, burly shore men practically ran them over with a cart they were pushing onto the ship. They obviously were on a mission and they moved about like they had done this before. This is it. This is the handoff of the cache. I'm sure of it.

Rico waves a flag from the upper deck. That's the signal to the shore patrol. Wait, Rose and I are still on board. We haven't gotten off yet. We're not supposed to be on the ship when this all comes down. Too late. Rico meets the authorities on the gang plank and escorts them directly to the Captain's quarters. They bust the door open and there they are. The Captain and the kitchen witch are packing up hundreds of plastic bags full of little white pills. Before I can stop her, Rose starts running toward Rico. "Rose, stop!" "Come back!" "No." "Maggie the Captain has a gun." "Rico, look out!"

The Captain takes aim at Rico just as Rose steps in front of him. I hear the gunshot and see Rose fall. Oh my God. Rose is shot. Rico carries Rose out of the cabin as the port police pull their guns and fire back at the Captain, and the two goons who decided to get in this gunfight. It's six to one and the Captain has no way out. I hear what sounds like the shooting range in the jail. Guns are going off everywhere around us. My first thought is Rose. God, please let her be alright. She is lying on the deck and Rico is holding her. All I see is the blood. She is bleeding badly and it looks like she took a shot to the chest. "Rose, can you hear me?" "Rose talk to me." "Tell me you're going to be alright." "Rose, please say something." It's suddenly silent. The guns have stopped. I don't hear anything. I can't say anything. All I see is my baby sister lying in a pool of blood.

"Maggie, get out of the way." "Let the ambulance crew get her to the hospital." I step back as Rose is lifted onto a gurney and rushed into an ambulance. I'm going with her. No one's going to stop me. Rose is the only thing that matters at this moment. I have no idea what else is happening. I find myself being shaken and rattled inside an ambulance that is speeding down the winding, bumpy streets of Antigua. The EMT's are working on Rose. I am praying. I know enough from my Red Cross training that Rose is in trouble. Her blood pressure is dropping and her pulse is weak. After what seemed like hours riding in the ambulance, we pull into the hospital ER drive. A crew comes running out to bring Rose in for evaluation. I don't feel very good about this island hospital, but it's our only option. I have to put Rose in the care of God and trust that He will bring her through. As they wheel her in, I am immediately directed to wait. So I waited. Waited in the ER waiting room. Waited in the hospital lunch room. Waited in the doorway. Waited in the outside sitting area. Waiting is not my forte. I am always the one who jumps into action. I always have to take control. But I was powerless. There was nothing I could do but wait and pray. They were operating on Rose to save her life. It's been hours that they've been working on her and I still don't know what's going on. It's maddening. My mind is reeling and I can't help but think about Tracey and Jill. It was only eight days ago that we were all in the emergency room, hoping they would survive.

Chapter Twenty-Four

"Well, I tried reaching Maggie, but I just got her answering machine. I did leave her a message to let her know that you guys are anxious to see her when she gets home." "Okay, that's great Tony. Thanks."

"What are you two up to today?" "We went to physical therapy together and had lunch just a little while ago." "Rumor has it, that we may be released tomorrow." "Wow. That's fantastic." "I'll make arrangements to be here to pick you up and take you both home tomorrow." "I appreciate that Tony, but let's try and confirm with the doctor before you put in for the time off." "Don't worry about that Tracey. Duff told me I can take any time I need. It won't be a problem." "That's awfully kind of him." "Please tell him we really appreciate his concern." "It's not only Duff. The whole building has been asking about you two. I don't think there is anyone who hadn't heard about the accident, and believe me, everyone is concerned." "You guys have a lot of friends whether you know it or not." "I can't wait to get back to work Tony." "I am bored out of my mind here." "Hey, not so fast." "Just because you're going home, doesn't mean you will be allowed to return to work yet." "I'm sure that's at least a few more weeks away." "Besides, you don't want to try and maneuver with those crutches in the jail. That's just not going to work." "Why not?" "I'll have a new weapon to protect myself from those inmates." "You're going to have to be patient. No one wants you rushing back before you are ready."

"You have additional surgeries scheduled for the plastic surgery on your face you know." "Oh yeah. I keep forgetting about that until I catch a glimpse of myself in the mirror." I guess you're right." "I'm really not ready for anyone at work to see the way I look right now." "You look gorgeous to me kid." "I hope you know I'm here for you." "I'm not going anywhere." "You are not going to be able to shake me." "I'm in for the long haul if you'll have me." "Tony, I can't think about that right now." "I just have to get through all this physical therapy and reconstructive surgery." "That's enough to challenge my psyche right now." "Long term is not in my view at the moment." "I get it Tracey." "Just please know I've got your back. Whatever you need." "I know Tony." "I can't thank you enough." "I never would have made it through this far without you." "Why don't you see if you can hunt down my doctor and find out if tomorrow is our release day." "The anticipation is killing me." "On my way."

Chapter Twenty-Five

It's been six hours and I'm still waiting. My head is about to explode when I see Rico busting into the waiting room. "Where's Rose?" "She's still in surgery." "She's been in there since they brought her in here." "Do you have an update?" "No nothing. I know nothing. I've been going out of my mind waiting here by myself. I am really glad to see you Rico." "I'm not sure I care anymore, but tell me what happened after we rushed out of there in the ambulance."

"The shore patrol was awesome. They took down those two hoods that came on board the ship, as well as the Captain and the kitchen witch. They are all in handcuffs at the Antigua Police Station, waiting transport to Miami. The DEA is taking over now. They could not believe the arrest we made with this gang of drug runners. They've been after them for a couple years. They suspected The Phantom was making those drug runs, but they could never prove anything." "They told me we are responsible for taking $25 Million worth of opioids out of the black market." "It's their biggest score yet." "You will see the news in The Antigua Observer tomorrow." "They even took my picture to run with the article." "Really?" "That's great Rico." "So our plan paid off." "I told them Maggie, that it was all you." "You were the one that picked up on the whole operation. You were the one who planned the whole sting." "They know all about you." "They might even try to reach you for an interview." "My only concern is Rose right now Rico." "I'll leave it to the DEA to handle things from here." "I've got bigger worries." "I know Maggie. I'm worried sick about Rose." "I love her Maggie." "Please Rico. Don't even say that to me." "I have loved and taken care of Rose all my life." "You don't know what it means to love her." "Yes I do Maggie." "I love Rose and I intend to make her mine." "I know she's going to pull through this, and when she does, I'm going to ask her to marry me." "Well, you better say your prayers Rico." "She's got a long way to go."

After three more rosaries and two hours later, the doctor finally comes out to talk to us. Rose made it through. The bullet missed her heart but went through her lung and imbedded in her chest wall. The doctor was able to remove it, but the path to finding it left a lot of damage along the way. Rose is still critical in ICU and the next 24 hours will determine if she has the strength and endurance to come through this ordeal. I wish I could trade places with her. I cannot stand the thought of life without Rose.

I'm going to stay right here in case she wakes up. I don't want her to feel scared and alone without me. I'm calling on all the saints in heaven now. Anybody and everybody upstairs have got to come to the rescue. Rico is at my side, praying along with me as we count down the hours to Rose being out of the woods. It's going to be a long night.

Chapter Twenty-Six

I wake up in the visitors lounge to Rico shaking me. I must have fallen asleep sometime during the night. I have no idea what time it is. Rico tells me that the nurse came in to tell us that Rose seems to be waking up. Our prayers have been heard. We burst into Rose's room in time to see her open her eyes. We are the first thing she sees. Me and Rico on either side of her. Both of us so thankful that she is looking at us. She's not speaking and seems to be having a hard time focusing. She knows we are with her, but she immediately goes back into unconsciousness. The doctor comes into the room to give us her prognosis. "Your little sister has a mighty spirit Maggie! She's definitely going to make it." "We had difficulty getting to the bullets." "Bullets?" "Yes Maggie, she took two to the chest." "It is amazing that they did not hit her heart. But they didn't." "Thank God Doctor." "What did they damage then?" "Her left lung was punctured and as a result deflated." "That was our biggest challenge in surgery." "The other bullet embedded in the back of her chest wall." "We were able to remove both bullets and get the lung inflated again." "She is breathing normally with the help of a little extra oxygen." "She is going to need extensive rehabilitation and recovery time. I don't see her able to travel back home for at least a week or so." "Once she gets home, she will need to continue working with doctors at the Clinic." "They will oversee her recovery which should take at least four months." "I have a call into a colleague of mine, Dr. Weiss. He intends to take on her case and I'm sure he will take good care of her. He's a good guy Maggie. You'll like him." "Hey, if he can help Rose, he'll be my new best friend."

Rico and I head down to the hospital cafeteria to grab something to eat. Not only are we both exhausted, we are starving too. Compared to what we've been eating on the ship for the last week, this cafeteria food looks gourmet to me. Scrambled eggs and sausage never tasted so good. And a cup of strong, hot coffee. Finally. We are not even half way through our breakfast when a group of people come bounding into the cafeteria. They spot us and immediately head right for us. Oh no! It's a news crew. Before we knew it, we were being bombarded with questions from reporters with The Antigua Observer, the Guatemala Telegraph, and The Associated Press. Plus they all had their own photographers in tow. The story got out somehow, and the newspapers were anxious to run with it. They could not have caught me at a worse moment with their cameras, but there was no escaping their pursuit. Rico and I were thrown into notoriety. We were hearing words like heroes, brave and daring. I really wanted no part of this but Rico seemed to be enjoying the attention. The next morning we awoke to being front page news. The Irish Corrections Officer and the local Ship Security Officer teaming up to make the biggest drug bust in Caribbean history. Like it or not, we were celebrities. I guess I'll never be able to take an anonymous vacation to the Caribbean ever again! Oh well. After this trip, I don't care if I ever see these islands again, I'll tell you that!

The next morning I grabbed a few copies of the newspapers to pack in my suitcase. Then I put one in my purse as I left to go to the hospital to check on Rose. Rico was already there when I got there, holding her hand and stroking her hair. They really did look like a couple in love.

"Hi there Ms. Hero!" I guess Rico got the newspapers to Rose already. She was speaking very softly and with great effort, but she was speaking. This made me feel so relieved. Rose was awake and talking. She looked awful, but that was beside the point. She made it. My baby sister was going to go home with me. At some point.

Chapter Twenty-Seven

Tony, Tracey, and Jill were driving home from the hospital when they heard a news report about a big drug bust in Antigua. They looked wide-eyed at each other and could not believe what they were hearing. "Corrections Officer, Margaret Flannery teamed up with the Ship's Security Officer, Rico Martin in planning and pulling off the capture and arrest of the king pin leaders of a worldwide opioid cartel."

"Oh my God. They're talking about Maggie!" "Turn it up Tony."

So, the news reached home before we did. Even on vacation I managed to get myself involved in trouble. The problem was, I still had to stay down in Antigua until Rose was well enough to travel home. That would be another two weeks at least. Day after day she was improving. She was still extremely weak and didn't seem to be eating much of anything. She said she just had no appetite. She could not entirely straighten up and she was walking with a walker. She was still in great pain. I felt horrible for her. Rico never left her side which was easy for him since he no longer had a job to go to everyday. Suddenly finding himself unemployed, he was very worried about his future. Knowing that he planned to propose to Rose, I could understand his concern.

I was finally starting to get my head together and I started thinking about my job. I guess I better try and get a hold of Duff, especially since I've been gone two weeks longer than I expected to be. I sure hope my job is not in jeopardy. The more I thought about it, the more nervous I got. I had to find a phone.

"County Sheriff's Office. This is Sgt. Duff speaking." "Duff, it's me Maggie." "Maggie! Where are you?" "Are you home yet?" "We all heard about what happened in Antigua." "Is your sister okay?" "Well, that's why I'm calling you Duff." "She took two bullets to the chest and she's in pretty bad shape." "She's going to recover, but it's going to take some time. I'm probably going to have to stay down here another two weeks at least." "Don't sweat it Maggie." "You do what you need to do there for your sister." "Just give me a call when you get back in town and we'll put you back on the schedule." "Duff, I cannot thank you enough." "It's been really crazy down here and I can't wait to get home and back to work." "Well, don't rush it Maggie. You take care of Rose and we'll see you later."

Okay. That's one worry off my mind. I better call Ma again. I didn't have much time to talk to her when I called her the night Maggie got shot. I know she must be worried sick. I sent her into a panic with my phone call and I need to give her an update on Maggie.

"Hi Ma. It's Maggie." "Saints in heaven Maggie. I've been worried sick about you and Rose. Why haven't you called me back sooner?" "I'm sorry Ma. It's just been so crazy down here. You have no idea what we've been through." "No, that's the point Maggie. I have no idea." "Listen Ma, Rose is doing well. She is up and walking around. She's still very weak, but she is recovering. She's going to be okay Ma." "Thank God!" "I haven't stopped praying since you called me." "I put the whole family on the prayer line and I've had Fr. Quinn mentioning her at Mass every day. "Well, your prayers have worked Ma. Rose is going to be just fine." "When do you think you girls will be getting home?" "That's up to her doctors Ma. We have to wait until she gets released to travel. I'm thinking it might be another couple weeks." "Well, I can wait as long as I know you's are coming." "We are Ma. We are."

Chapter Twenty-Eight

Tony pulls into the driveway, and Tracey starts to lose it. She is shaking and crying uncontrollably. Jill jumps out of the back seat and gets a hold of Tracey. She is hugging her for a good ten minutes before Tracey starts to calm down. "What is it Tracey?" "What's wrong? Why are you so upset?" "I'm home now Tony." "How am I supposed to go back to my life?" "How can I go back to work?" "You know I have to work." "I'm on my own." "I need my job." "Well first of all you are not on your own Tracey. You have Jill and you have me." "We are not going anywhere."

Tony has his arm around Tracey as they approach the side door of the house. Jill went ahead and got the house open and the lights on. They slowly walk up the steps and into the house. Tracey heads straight for her favorite rocking chair. "Oh my gosh! I can't believe how much I've missed this chair!" "This chair is home to me. I've finally made it home." "Can you let me just sit here and rock a bit Tony?" "I just want to look around and get my head on straight." "Take your time Tracey."

"Jill and I are going to make us all a cup of tea." "Would you like that?" "Yes, please. That would be great! Thank you."

Tony joins Jill in the kitchen just as the kettle starts whistling. "Hey, listen, Jill, after we finish our tea I would appreciate it if you would find a reason to leave. I want to be alone with Tracey for a bit if you don't mind." "Well, I guess so Tony, but for how long?" "I don't want Tracey to think I am abandoning her." "I'll want to come back as soon as possible." "Why do you have to be alone with her?" "I think the more people she has around her right now, the better off she'll be." "Just trust me on this will you please Jill?" "You can come back in a couple hours." "Okay. I need to pick up her prescriptions at the drug store anyway, so I'll tell her that's where I'm going. I also need to pick up a few groceries since there is little to no food in this house." "Those sound like legitimate errands don't they Tony?" "Yes Jill, that's perfect." "I really appreciate this. Thanks so much." "Okay, so it's 5:30 right now. I'll be back by 7:30." "Does that give you enough time to do whatever it is you want to do?" "Yes Jill, that will work. Thank you so much!"

Jill brings a tray with the tea cups and cookies into the living room where Tracey is rocking away in her chair. She offers a cup to Tracey who immediately takes a sip and smiles. "That's what we like to see Tracey." "It's so great to see you home." "You and Tony enjoy your tea, I've got to run out and get your prescriptions at the drug store and pick up some groceries so you don't starve to death in this house. " "I'll be back in a couple hours." "Okay Jill, but please be careful. Are you sure you don't want Tony to go with you?" "No that's okay Tracey. I'll be just fine I promise." I don't want to leave you alone so just visit with

Tony here while I'm gone. " "Well okay, but hurry back. I miss you already."

Jill drives away in Tony's car while he settles into a chair right next to Tracey's. "How do you feel Babe?" "I feel really glad to be home Tony. I don't think I could have stood one more night in that hospital." "I never could have gone through it all without you Tony." "I hope you know how much I appreciate everything you've done for me." "No need for thanks Babe." "You know I would walk through a wall for you if I had to." "I do know that Tony." "You are the best." "Hold that thought Tracey." "Over these past couple months, I've come to realize just how much I miss being married to you." "Being together with you makes me feel whole again." "I've never stopped loving you Tracey." "I hope you know that." "Well, I've managed to figure that one out Tony since you haven't left my side since the accident." "I'm being serious here Tracey." "Please hear me out." "What?" "What are you trying to say Tony?" "I'm trying to tell you that I've never loved you more than I do right now and I would be honored if you would consider being my wife again." "You're asking me to marry you again?" "Really?" "I don't need your pity Tony." "I know what I look like, and this face is not the one you married ten years ago." "Your face is the only face I need to have in my life Tracey." "You are more beautiful to me now than you've ever been." "It's not pity in my heart for you, it's a love so deep and consuming that I just have to have you back in my life. And I mean permanently this time."

"I love you more now than ever." "I am asking you to marry me Tracey." "Would you...please?"

"Tony, I don't know what to say." "I am so grateful to you for everything." "I'll admit that being together with you through this whole ordeal has made me feel closer to you than anyone ever has." "I do love you Tony." "There is a part of me that always will, now more than ever." "I just don't know if I'm ready to commit to marriage again." "I need some time to see how I feel as I continue to recover." "Please understand." "I'm not saying no." "I just need to think this through." "I need to get back to work and get my life back on track." "Can you give me some time Tony?" "Can you do that for me?" "Anything you say Tracey." "I think you know that by now." "I'll do anything you say."

Chapter Twenty-Nine

She opens her eyes to a sunny bright room filled with flowers. Roses. Every color of the rainbow. They're everywhere! Red Roses, Yellow Roses, White Roses, Pink Roses, Lilac Roses. The room is absolutely bursting with roses. "Maggie, where did all these roses come from?" "I'm not sure Rose." "When I got here this morning the room looked just like this." "I'm surprised the fragrance didn't wake you up earlier. It smells like a funeral home in here." "Let's not go there Maggie. "How are you feeling today?" "Well, at the moment, pretty good." "I would like to sit up in that chair if you wouldn't mind helping me." "Sure Rose." "Let me get your walker over here and I'll help you walk over there."

Just as Rose starts trying to get up from the bed, Rico comes flying into the room. "No, no my sweet." "Let me carry you over there." He sweeps her up into his arms like a child and gently lowers her into the leather recliner that was in the corner of the room. "How do you like your flowers Rose?" "Roses for my Rose!" "So these are all from you Rico?" "Of course, my love." "I am so happy that you are alive and getting better!" "We need to celebrate." "We need to appreciate all the beautiful things in life." "To me, there is nothing more beautiful than my Rose." Rico gets down on his knee and kisses Rose. "Rose, I need you in my life." "I have never felt so alive, so vital, so loved, since I met you." "You are what's been missing in my life and I will never let you go." "Marry me Rose." "Be my wife so we can be together forever." With that Rico pulls out a diamond ring. "What do you say Rose?" "You can make me the happiest man alive." "Will you say yes?"

"I'm feeling pretty awkward over here you guys." "I think I'm going to go get a cup of coffee while you talk this over." "Okay Maggie." "Thanks."

Rico looks into Rose's eyes with the passion of a man in love. He strokes her hair as he gently hugs her, careful not to lean on her chest. "My darling Rose." "You are everything I could hope for in life." "I love you with all my heart and I promise to treasure you forever." "Please be mine."

"Rico, I feel the same way about you." "I was afraid to admit that to myself, because I was sure we had to go our separate ways." "I will be yours Rico. I do say yes. I want you in my life forever too." "But what do we do now?" "You know I have to go home once I can travel again." "Are you going to come back to Cleveland with me?" "Yes, of course Rose." "I need to be where you are, no matter where that is." "Even Cleveland." "I have no reason to stay in Antigua now." "I have no job." "I'm not sure what I'll do in Cleveland, but I'll work out something. Don't worry Rose, we will be just fine as long as we have each other." "I truly believe that Rico." "I know everything will work out. We just have to have faith in each other." "I'm not sure how Maggie is going to take this though." "Maybe you should leave before she comes back so I can talk to her alone." "Of course Rose." "You break the news to Maggie, and I'll be back in a couple hours." "I love you my darling." "I love you too Rico. I can't believe this is happening, but I am so happy."

Rose is sitting in the recliner with her feet up as Maggie comes back into her room. Rose is smiling from ear to ear and Maggie knows what's coming. "So did you say yes Rose?" "Did you agree to marry him?" Rose extends her left arm out to show Maggie the diamond on her finger. "Well I guess that answers my question." "But tell me this, Rose." "How do you think you guys are going to make it?" "Rico doesn't even have a job. How is he going to support you?" "I really don't know right now Maggie, but I do know that we'll figure it out together." "I have never felt more sure about anything in my life Maggie." "I know Rico and I are meant to be together forever and nothing is going to get in the way of our sharing our lives together." "Not even you." "Listen Rose, I'm not trying to get in your way here." "I'm just pointing out the obvious. I'm asking the questions you know Ma is going to ask." "How are you going to face her and tell her that you plan to marry an unemployed native of Antigua?" "That's bound to get her Irish up!" "You'll have to help me through that Maggie." "You know Ma will look to you to see what you think of all this." "If she knows you are okay with it, then she'll accept it." "We'll see about that one Rose." I know you and Rico are crazy about each other, but you've only known him for a week. "I'm sure there's a lot you don't know about him." "Well, that's true Maggie, but there's a lot he doesn't know about me either." "We are just going to have to trust each other."

"I had a talk with your doctor while I was gone getting coffee. He tells me that you are going to be released tomorrow and that you will be able to fly home as long as you see your doctor in Cleveland as soon as possible." "Oh my God, Maggie." "That's wonderful." "Wait till I tell Rico." "Yeah, and speaking of, should I book him a ticket to Cleveland too?" "He'll be back here in a little while." "Let me give him the good news and see what he wants to do." "Okay you do that." "I'm going to go back to the hotel and start packing up our stuff."

Chapter Thirty

Tracey and Jill show up for roll call on the same day. Duff knew they were coming back, but none of the other CO's did. Tony, of course, was right beside Tracey. His posture and demeanor were just daring anyone to say anything about Tracey's face. He was ready to jump down the throat of anyone who could be that stupid. Once roll call was over, Tracey and Jill were surrounded by everyone there. Everyone was so happy to see them back, there wasn't one ugly comment made. The hugging went on for quite a while until the alarm went off. There was a situation in pod #72. Two inmates were going at each other and the blood was flying. The CO's go running to the pod and break things up before anyone was seriously hurt. "Well I guess things haven't changed much huh Jill?" "No Tracey." "That's kind of comforting in a weird sort of way." "I know what you mean. I was thinking the same thing."

"I hear everyone is going to Dugan's when our shift is over to celebrate our return." "Guess it wouldn't be much of a celebration if we didn't show up." "Are you going to feel like going?" "Yeah, I really do want to try and normalize my life as much as possible." "Stopping for a beer after shift is pretty normal, don't you think Jill?" "Yeah, I guess I'll go too if you're going." "I know Tony will be there." "He's not letting you out of his sight." "You've noticed that too huh?" "Oh yeah. So, have you come to any decision on his proposal yet?" "I have Tracey." "In fact, I plan to let him know tonight at Dugan's what I've decided." "So no preview for me huh?" "Nope, sorry Jill." "You're going to have to wait on this till I've talked things through with Tony. You understand don't you Jill?" "Of course. I get it." "But I'm going to be the first in line to hear the news after you talk to Tony right?" "Yes Jill, I promise, you'll be the second one to know."

Dugan's is jammed. Mostly with CO's. Jill and Tracey are sitting at the bar when Tony walks in. It was starting to feel like the old days. And Tracey was feeling pretty good about that. Tony sits down on the stool next to Tracey just as she is getting up. "I'll be right back Tony." "I need to visit the restroom." "Ok Babe, I'll be waiting right here for you."

"So Jill, what do you know?" "What do you mean, what do I know? What do you know?" "I don't know anything and it's making me crazy." Tony takes a sip of his beer and suddenly hears a familiar tune on the juke box. It's Elvis. Tracey's favorite. There she is, standing next to the juke box looking at Tony with her hand held out. Tony makes a beeline for her and they begin to dance.

Wise men say, only fools rush in, but I can't help falling in love with you. "Tony, are you listening to the words of this song?" "I don't need to listen to the words Tracey, I know this song by heart." "What are you trying to tell me Babe?" "I think this song says it all Tony, let's just dance." Tony holds her close as the tears stream down his face. He can't help himself. His dream is coming true. She's saying yes. Yes to having him back in her life as her husband. They dance to the end of the song and then Tony immediately gets on his knees. He's kneeling right in front of Tracey with the biggest diamond ring she's ever seen. "Tracey, will you marry me, again?" "Yes Tony, I will marry you again." "This time it better be for good." "Oh it will be Babe. Don't worry, it will be."

Chapter Thirty-One

Rose and Rico are in the back seat of the cab and I'm jammed in the front with the driver, his newspapers, his lunch, his radio, and his filthy dirty duffle bag that contains who knows what. And I really don't want to know. The romance radiating from the back seat is a bit sickening, but I'm toughing through it. My mind is focused on getting us home.

We get through the ticket line and are directed to the Custom's booth. So now we are travelling back home with a foreigner to the U.S. and one of us who only has a baptismal certificate for identification as a U.S. citizen. We pick the line that has the least intimidating looking officer. Well, you know the old saying; don't judge a book by its cover.

Rose goes first. She smiles and hands the officer her baptismal certificate. "Oh, so you're Catholic huh?" "That's nice." Go right ahead miss. Now it's Rico's turn. Because of his job on the cruise ship, he has an official Antiguan passport. The official actually recognizes him as a frequent traveler. "Hey Rico, how's it going?" "You going to America this time?" "Yeah, for good." "Really?" "Does that have anything to do with that little lady I just passed through?" "Oh yeah man!" "She's going to be my wife."

"That's fantastic man, congratulations." "Thanks buddy. I'm on top of the world right now."

Now it's my turn. I present my official birth certificate to the customs agent. "Is this all you have ma'am? " "Yes, that's all I have. What's the problem? It worked fine for me to get into your country. Why won't it work for me to leave?" "How do I know this is you?" "I have no picture on this document." "This could belong to anybody." "Where did you go to high school?" "Really, you're asking me where I went to high school? You wouldn't know if I told you." "Well, I'm still asking! Where did you go to high school?" "Oh, for God's sake. I went to West Tech in Cleveland, Ohio." "Does that mean anything to you now?" "No it does not ma'am." "I'm going to have to ask you to step aside." "You will be detained her for a bit until I can verify your identify." "My identity?" "Hey, I work in the criminal justice system. I am a Corrections Officer for the County of Cuyahoga, in Cleveland, Ohio." "You can call the Sheriff himself, and he'll tell you who I am. I am Sgt. Maggie Flannery, that's who." "You've got your nerve buddy."

As the volume of the conversation went up, Rose and Rico notice what's going on with Maggie. "Frederico, Frederico, I know this lady." "She is with us." "This is my sweetheart's sister Maggie." "You mean she's with you Rico?" "Yes Frederico, she is with me." "Please let her through." "I'm telling you she is who she says she is. You really don't want to mess with her."

"Okay Rico, if you say so, I will let her through." "So you can guarantee me she is not a threat?" "Well, I can't guarantee that Frederico, but I'm telling you, you need to let her pass through. Please." "Ok Miss Maggie." "If Rico says you are good to go, then you are good to go."

We finally get on our plane, headed for Miami. Our layover is pretty tight, so I hope we don't have any hold-ups there. I've had just about all I can stand.

Once again I am crammed into a seat with about six inches of leg room. And this time I am seated next to a stranger. Rose and Rico are seated together behind me. Nothing bothers them in their state of unrequited love. We cannot get to Miami fast enough as far as I am concerned. I really need to put this trip behind me and get on with my boring, but safe routine. I am carefully nursing my sunburned neck, arms, and legs. All the sunscreen in the world is not enough to protect this milk white Irish skin. The burning and itching is enough to drive me to jump out this plane window. If only I could. I really don't know what's worse. The pain and itch of my sunburn, or the conversation I can't help but hear going on behind me. I guess I better get used to Rose and Rico being together. I don't like feeling like a third wheel all the time, and I miss alone time with my sis. But this union is moving forward no matter how I feel about it. I just hope it works out alright for Rose. I swear I will kill him if he hurts her in any way.

Chapter Thirty-Two

Finally, I can see the Miami sky line. Can't wait to land back in the good old USA. I can tell our plane is approaching the landing strip too fast, and sure enough we have a bang down landing. But we're down, we made it. Hallelujah! I try to stand up so I can gather my carry-on and jacket while I hear the cabin steward announcing that all luggage must be claimed at the baggage carousel because we must once again report in to Customs. Well at least this time, it's US Customs. I can get through this one last hurdle to home. I think.

I can barely walk down the roll-up stairs but I make it and begin the trek to baggage. I feel like I aged 10 years during this trip. I can't straighten up my back, and my legs are shaking as I try to walk through the airport. I'm never going to make it. "Hey Rose." "Let's get one of those courtesy carts to drive us to baggage." "I can't make it." "No worries Maggie", says Rico. "I'll get us one." "You stay here with Rose while I hunt one down." "Oh sure thing, wouldn't want anything to happen to

Rose now would we?" "What's wrong Maggie?" "Are you mad at me?" "No Rose." "I just want to get home."

Rico arrives on a cart and we are on our way to baggage claim. Carousel number 6. Well, that's appropriate. Why not number 6? That's been our number this whole trip.

After waiting what felt like an hour, the carousel starts to turn and the light is flashing. Here comes the luggage. Rose sees her bag right away. It is easily identified because of the Kelly Green scarf with shamrocks she has tied to the handle. One down. Next comes Rico's. His looks like the most well-traveled bag on the plane. Scuffed, torn, and with one broken wheel. He doesn't care. He's in love.

Okay that's two down. Now where's my bag? After another ten-minute wait, I see my bag coming down the chute. It is easily recognizable by the granny panties falling out as it goes around the carousel. Not only is the bag open, it's spilling out my clothes onto the baggage carousel and riding them around faster than I can catch it. Bras, underpants, swimsuits. God help me. I'm being exposed to the world here. This is someone's idea of a cruel joke. I go running to try and gather up all my unmentionables and get the bag off the belt. Nope. Miss it on the first try. It's going to go through the belt a second time. Wonderful! I can't believe this is happening. The entire airport is falling down laughing at this hysterical situation. Including Rose and Rico. Very funny guys. Don't just stand there laughing, help me! Rico goes into action and grabs the open bag on its second approach. Thank God. Now I have the public humiliation of stuffing all my dirty clothes back into the damn bag. Including the underpants that some man brings over to me asking, "Is this by chance yours?" Okay, the show's over folks!

Onto Customs for clearance into Miami, Florida, USA. Once again, Rose and Rico are passed through Customs without a hitch. I, of course, am questioned as if I am the head of an illegal drug cartel. I swear I must have the look of a criminal. I guess what I do for a living is rubbing off on me. I don't like it.

Chapter Thirty-Three

I can see the Terminal Tower, so I know we are about fifteen minutes to landing. I have never been so happy to see Cleveland, Ohio. We all exit the plane and proceed to the luggage claim area. As we reach the end of the concourse, I see the signs and hear the uproar. It's an army of County CO's with welcome signs and banners. And who's leading the charge but Duff, Tracey, Tony, Jill and Joan. They must have looked up our flight information so they could put together this welcome committee for our arrival. I can barely take it all in when some guy shoves a microphone in front of my face and asks me what it feels like to be a hero? A hero? What are you talking about? "It's been reported that you are responsible for the arrest of the most notorious boss of the Caribbean drug cartel." "Thanks to you there are going to be a lot less illegal opioids for sale on the streets of America." "How does that feel Ms. Flannagan?" "You have made a significant impact in the war on drugs." "Well, I'm glad to have done my part, but believe me I did not go on vacation asking for trouble." "I just reacted to a bad situation I saw unfolding in front of me." "It's in my nature to do the right thing. And this time, the right thing was a pretty big thing." "And I would like to introduce Mr. Rico Martin. You may also have heard that Mr. Martin was the Chief Security Officer on the ship where this all came down. It is thanks to Mr. Martin that I was able to plan and execute the arrest of the culprits in the drug ring. We acted as a team. He was integral to our success."

I finally shake the reporter as I approach my friends. They are all yelling and hugging me. I'm so happy to see them all. It's been six weeks since we left on that fateful cruise. Tracey shows me the diamond ring on her left hand. Tony is standing there shaking his head. Yes, yes, yes. We're going to get married again Maggie. Can you believe it? I am so happy I am going to have my Tracey back in my life. She is standing there next to him. As beautiful as ever! I can see some faint scaring on her face and she is walking with a very subtle limp, but I can tell she has come back from a trip to hell and is well on her way to complete recovery.

"Tracey, I am so happy for you." "Can you ever forgive me for going on this trip while you were so hurt from the accident?" "Maggie, please don't worry about it. I would have done the exact same thing. There was nothing you could have done anyway and I'm glad you didn't lose all your money." "We heard you brought your sister with you." "Is this her?" "Yes Tracey, meet Rose." "Rose went on the cruise with me and she got way more than a vacation out of the deal." "She's now engaged to Rico, who she met while onboard the ship." "Wow, so that's two engagements that happened while you were gone."

Chapter Thirty-Four

Duff brought one of the County vans to the airport so he could give us a ride home. He is so proud of me and he told me he is so happy that I'll be coming back to work very soon. I guess the fun at the facility has not stopped in my absence and he says he could really use the iron fist of Maggie Flannery back in the jail. Oh well, somebody loves me! I don't really want to think about that homecoming until we get past the first one coming up momentarily with Ma.

Duff pulls the van in the driveway, and I see the curtain in the window pulled back. There's Ma looking out at us waving. She meets us at the door with open arms. "Thank God you girls are back." "I was beginning to think I would never see you again." "We're back Ma, and you wouldn't believe the trip we had." "It was one fiasco after another." "I've never been so happy to be home." "And who is this fella Rose?" "Ma, meet Rico." "We're engaged to be married." "Saints in Heaven Rose, what are you talking about? You leave on vacation and come back engaged?" "After all you've been through, are you sure this is the right thing to do?" "Maybe your emotions are leading you down a path here that you haven't explored quite enough yet." "No Ma." "This is the real thing. Rico has not left my side since I got shot." "He has taken such good care of me and I love him with all my heart." "Well love doesn't put food on the table Rose. Forgive me if I act like your mother here, but I understand he doesn't even have a job right now." "How do you think you two are going to make it?" "That's not a very good way to start out a marriage."

"Well, that's not exactly true Ma." "What do you mean Maggie? What are you talking about?" "Rico has a job if he wants it." "I talked to Duff the last day we were in Antigua and explained how Rico lost his job because the ship he served on is now in Federal custody in a major criminal investigation." I explained how Rico worked with me to bring down the drug ring and I told Duff he is a stand-up guy with a strong background in security. He's proven himself to me as honest, capable, and someone I would be comfortable working with. All Rico has to do is go Downtown and fill out an application." "After a successful background check, the job is his. County CO."

"What?" "Is this true Maggie?" "You got me a job in America?" "Yes Rico, I got you a job in America." "If you're going to marry my little sister Rose, you better have means to support her."

"Maggie I can't believe you did that. You are the best!" "Thank you so much for helping Rico. This means the world to me."

"You mean the world to me Rose." "Let's not plan any more vacations together, okay?" "That Phantom Voyage is the last cruise I'll ever take!"